Frederic D. Huntington

Elim: or, Hymns of Holy Refreshment

Frederic D. Huntington

Elim: or, Hymns of Holy Refreshment

ISBN/EAN: 9783744773843

Printed in Europe, USA, Canada, Australia, Japan

Cover: Foto ©Andreas Hilbeck / pixelio.de

More available books at **www.hansebooks.com**

Elim:

OR

HYMNS OF HOLY REFRESHMENT.

EDITED BY THE

REV. F. D. HUNTINGTON, D. D.

" And they came to Elim, where were twelve wells of water, and threescore and ten palm-trees: and they encamped there by the waters."

BOSTON:
E. P. DUTTON AND COMPANY.
NEW YORK: HURD AND HOUGHTON.
1866.

RIVERSIDE, CAMBRIDGE:
STEREOTYPED AND PRINTED BY
H. O. HOUGHTON AND COMPANY.

> "They greet me midst the shadows cold,—
>   Such thoughts as holy men of old
>   Amidst the desert found;
>   Such gladness as in Him they felt
>   Who, with them, through the darkness dwelt
>   And compassed all around."
>
> RUSKIN.

PREFACE.

DRAWN from many sources, fugitive and permanent, old and new, near and distant, open and obscure, the contents of this volume cannot be better introduced than in the language of the Preface of the "Lyra Anglicana,"— from which some of the most striking and valued pieces are taken, — by the Rev. R. H. Baynes, M. A. of St. Edmund Hall, Oxford, and Perpetual Curate of Holy Trinity, Maidstone : —

"A few words will explain the object of this Collection of Hymns and Sacred Songs. It is intended as a supplement to the many books of a similar character already published. I have therefore purposely excluded many well-known and favorite hymns, on the ground that nearly all of them are to be found in those Collections to which I have referred. A considerable number of those inserted in this Book will be new to the majority of readers, but I venture to believe that, when known and appreciated, they will be added to the list of those Sacred Songs most dear to Christian hearts."

" It would be almost impossible to overrate the value of really good hymns for private as well as public use. Next to the Bible itself, hymns have done more to influence our views and mould our theology than any other instrumentality whatever. There is a power in hymns which never dies. Easily learned in the days of childhood and of youth ; often repeated ; seldom, if ever, forgotten, they abide with us, a most precious heritage, amid all the changes of our earthly life. They form a fitting and most welcome expression for every kind of deep religious feeling : they are with us to speak of Faith and Hope in hours of trial and sorrow ; with us, to animate to all earnest Christian effort ; with us, as the rich Consolation of individual hearts, and as one common bond of Fellowship between the living members of Christ's mystical body."

" If the present Collection should tend in any way to further these blessed ends, I shall indeed rejoice, and shall consider any labor on my part as more than abundantly repaid."

To this may be fitly added Milton's musical prose definition of the purposes of such poetry :

" To celebrate in glorious and lofty hymns the throne and equipage of God's almightiness ; and what He works, and what He suffers to be wrought with high providence in His Church ; to sing victorious agonies of saints and martyrs, the deeds and triumphs of just and pious nations doing valiantly, through faith, against Christ's enemies ; to deplore the general relapses of kingdoms and states from justice and God's true worship : Lastly, whatsoever in religion is holy and sublime ; in virtue, amiable or grave . . . . all these things to paint out and describe, teaching over the whole book of sanctity and virtue, through all the instances of example, with such delight to those especially of soft and delicious temper, who will not so much as look upon Truth herself unless they see her elegantly dressed, —that whereas the paths of honesty and good life appear now to be rugged and difficult, though they be indeed easy and pleasant, they will then appear to all men easy and pleasant, though they were rugged and difficult indeed."

The "Palms" of Elim stand for majesty, strength, and victory. The "Fountains" are for fruitfulness, beauty, and peace. These refreshing images represent the character of the grand and comforting compositions which are here brought together. Considering how rapidly the stores of Sacred verse — including some of a really high order of poetical and spiritual excellence — have accumulated in our language within a few years, by research and by production, it may not be thought presumptuous to say that it has been endeavored to admit no one poem into this Collection that does not bear some mark of poetic power and of a clear spiritual discernment. The compiler thinks, with equal confidence, that the whole volume will be found to be pervaded with the blessed Doctrine and Spirit of Christ, our Sacrifice and our Righteousness, — the indwelling Light and Eternal Life of believing souls.

F. D. H.

ALL SAINTS' DAY, 1864.

CONTENTS.

		Page
Reason and Faith	*C. F. Alexander*	1
Repentance and Faith	*Rev. W. Alexander*	3
Believers not seeing	*Canterbury Hymnal*	6
" I know in whom I have believed "		7
" Seek ye my face — Thy face, Lord, will I seek "	*E. K. Blunt*	9
Strength in Weakness	*C. L. Ford*	11
I said	*Caroline A. Mason*	13
The Compass		15
Mont Blanc revisited		16
My Sheep hear my Voice		18
The Shadow of a Great Rock in a Weary Land		20
This is my Beloved and this is my Friend	*S. Bernard*	23
O Lord, Thou knowest ! *Author of " Hymns from the Land of Luther "*		25
Rabbi, where dwellest Thou ? — Come and see *Author of the " Three Wakings "*		28
The Well at Sychar *Author of the " Three Wakings "*		30
Come, blessed Jesu		32
The Love of Christ which passeth Knowledge	*Christina G. Rossetti*	34
For us also	*John Wesley*	36
The Israelites at the Red Sea		38
The Way of Sorrows	*W. Chatterton Dix*	40

Contents.

Page

Emmaus . . . . Thomas Grinfield 42
Sunday Eve . . James D. Burns 44
At the Door . . . Joseph Grigg 46
Hymn for Epiphany . C. F. Alexander 48
Rest . . . . . "H. L. L." 49
" I am Thine " . . . . Gambold 51
Jesus is God ! . . . Oratory Hymns 53
Worthy the Lamb . Canterbury Hymnal 55
I will not let Thee go . . C. Wesley 57
The Boy with the Five Loaves Lyra Innocentium 59
Christ and the Little Ones 62
" My Meditation of Him shall be sweet " Toplady 65
" Christ in you, the Hope of Glory " . Toplady 68
Love of Love 69
" Come unto Me " . . Stephen of Saba 71
A Hymn of Angelus, of the Seventeenth Century
                                    C. Winkworth 73
Christ all in all . . . W. C. C. 75
Jesus passeth by . . C. A. M. W. 76
The Answer 78
Christ's Word, " Abide " . . . 80
Sunday next before Advent . . . 82
A Death-bed Hymn 83
The Three Wonders . W. Chatterton Dix 85
Come ! ye Lofty, Come ! ye Lowly Archer Gurney 87
The Infant Jesus . . Oratory Hymns 89
Midnight Christmas Communion . E. L. L. 91
A Carol for Christmas-tide . . A. M. M. 94
Good Friday . . Canterbury Hymnal 96
The Chastisement of our Peace was upon Him 98
A Fine Day in Passion Week Rev. W. Alexander 100
The Vigil . . . . Anna Shipton 102
Gethsemane . . . . Hart 104
An Ancient Hymn for Maunday-Thursday : from
    the German 107

Contents. xi

		Page
At the Lord's Feast	M. B. Wheaton	109
Touched with a Feeling of our Infirmities	C. F. Alexander	112
Not our Work		114
The Grief of Pleasures	Philip S. Worsley	115
The Healer	Canterbury Hymnal	117
" Made nigh by the Blood of Christ "	J. Wesley	119
Latus Salvatoris	M. Bridges	121
The Cross and the Heart		123
The Bread that cometh down from Heaven	C. Wadsworth	125
The Miracles of Grace and Nature	J. S. B. Monsell	127
The Christian Altar		129
The Oblation	Christina G. Rossetti	130
The Holy Feast	H. Alford	132
The Hunger	M. Bridges	133
The Morning of Reception	W. G. Tupper	134
This do in Remembrance of Me	Bonar	136
The True Bread	Bonar	139
And when they had sung an Hymn, they went out unto the Mount of Olives	Lyra Anglicana	141
Holy Communion	Richard Crashaw	143
Communion Hymn	C. F. Alexander	145
The Holy Communion	Author of the " Three Wakings "	148
The Completion of the Sacrifice of the Cross	A. M. M.	150
Rock of Ages — in Latin	Right Hon. W. L. Gladstone	152
Easter-Eve	Archer Gurney	154
Vigil of Easter-Eve	Child's Christian Year	156
Christ risen	Canterbury Hymnal	158
Easter Day	Lyra Anglicana	160
Hymn for Easter	Bonar	162
Easter Celebration	W. B.	165

Page

Ascension . . . *Canterbury Hymnal* 167
The Ceaseless Intercession . . *C. S.* 169
Homeward Guide . . *Arthur Tozer Russell* 171
The Lord's Knocking . . *Herbert Kynaston* 172
How long ?
    Author of " Hymns from the Land of Luther " 174
Behold, the Bridegroom cometh . . *Laurenti* 176
Hymn for Advent . . . *C. F. Alexander* 178
The Blessed Hope . *Rev. H. G. Tomkins* 180
Even so come, Lord Jesus . . . *Bonar* 181
Surely I come quickly . *John S. B. Monsell* 183
Lighted Lamps . . *Canterbury Hymnal* 184
The Second Advent 186
A Litany to the Holy Ghost . *Herrick* 187
The Spirit also helpeth our Infirmities
    Rev. H. G. Tomkins 188
Lead me and guide me . . *Newman* 190
Daily Service of the Church . . . 191
On hearing Week-day Service at Westminster Abbey, Sept. 1858 . . . *S. F.* 194
Jacob's Ladder . *Rev. W. Alexander* 197
The Lord's Day . . *Sir E. B. Lytton* 199
Hymn for All Saints' Day *Rev. H. G. Tomkins* 201
The Burial of Moses . *C. F. Alexander* 203
Vision from the Apocalypse *Rev. W. Alexander* 207
White Robes and Palms *Child's Christian Year* 210
Before the Throne . *Canterbury Hymnal* 212
" That where I am ye may be also " . . 215
Athanasius against the World
    Rev. W. R. Huntington 217
Faith . . . . *Miss Noble* 219
She hath done what she could . . *C. L. Ford* 222
Behold, I stand at the Door and knock *A. C. Coxe* 224
The Sun of Righteousness . *C. F. Alexander* 226
The Wanderer . . . *E. L. Lee* 229

Page

" Who can forgive Sins, but God only ? " . . 231
Kyrie Eleison . . *Catherine Winkworth* 233
I believe in the Resurrection of the Body
        A. L. Waring 235
The Widow of Nain .. . *W. R. Neale* 238
The Grave at Bethany . . *C. L. Ford* 241
The Maid is not dead, but sleepeth . . 244
Strangers and Sojourners . *Canterbury Hymnal* 247
Below and above . . *Rev. W. Alexander* 248
Now is our Salvation nearer than when we believed
        Carey 252
The Death of the Christian *Rev. J. D. Burns* 254
Who, and whence 256
Only waiting 259
Going Home . . . *Lyra Anglicana* 261
The Jerusalem that is above . *S. Bernard* 263
No Night there . . *Canterbury Hymnal* 268
" Thou art my Portion, O Lord " . . 270
" Till the Change come " . . . 271
The Mount of Olives . . *C. L. Ford* 275
A Prayer 278
Rest and Peace in Truth *Adelaide A. Procter* 280
Here is 'my Heart 281
A Soul's Entreaty 284
Evening Hymn of the Greeks . *Anatolius* 286
Even-song . . . *Lyra Anglicana* 287
Lighten our Darkness . *Lyra Anglicana* 290
An Evening Hymn . . *Oratory Hymns* 291
Midnight 293
Morning . . *Hymnologia Christiana* 295
Prayer for the Gift of Gratitude . . 297
In all Time of our Prosperity *Edward C. Porter* 298
Aspiration 301
Day and Night *Rev. John S. B. Monsell, LL. D.* 303
Discouraged because of the Way *Christian Lyrics* 305

Contents.

		Page
The Maid in Syria .	*Child's Christian Year*	311
One by one . . .	*A. A. Procter*	313
They that sow in Tears shall reap in Joy		
	Author of the " Three Wakings "	315
Christ at Sychar . . .	*Lyra Anglicana*	317
The Sages and the Shepherds . . .		319
As one whom his Mother comforteth		
	Lucy F. M. Mayo	320
Something for Thee		322
The Carver's Lesson		324
Marah and Elim		327

Credo.

REASON AND FAITH.

THROUGH paths of pleasant thought I
    ran,
    False science sang enchanted airs;
She told of nature and of man,
    And of the Godlike gifts he bears.
But when I sat down by the way,
    And thought out life, and thought out sin,
The burning truths that round me lay,
    And all the weak, proud self within;

Still in my single soul there wrought
    The sense of sin, the curse of doom,
'Till slowly broke upon my thought
    An Eastern olive-garden's gloom.
Hung on Thy Cross 'twixt earth and heaven
    I saw Thee, Son of man Divine;
To Thee the bitter pain was given,
    But all the heavy guilt was mine.

I know the serpent touched my heart,
　I saw his trail on hand and brow;
No sinless thought, no perfect part,
　But sullied breast and broken vow.
But then I felt my need of Thee,
　And pride's illusions passed away;
And oh! that Thou hast died for me,
　Is more than all the world can say.

The wounded fawn in yonder glade,
　Beside the doe seeks rest from harm;
The babe that scorned its mother's aid
　Flies to her at the least alarm.
And thus I feel my need of Thee,
　When sin and pride would tempt me most;
And oh! that Thou hast died for me,
　Is more than all the sceptic's boast.

REPENTANCE AND FAITH.

" Repentance toward God, and faith toward our Lord
Jesus Christ."

THERE was a ship, one eve autumnal, onward
    Steered o'er an ocean lake, —
Steered by some strong hand ever as if sun-
    ward ;
    Behind an angry wake,
Before there stretched a sea that grew intenser,
    With silver fire far spread,
Up to a hill mist-gloried, like a censer,
    With smoke encompassèd ;
It seemed as if two seas met brink to brink,
A silver flood beyond a lake of ink.

There was a soul that eve autumnal sailing
    Beyond the earth's dark bars,
Toward the land of sunsets never paling,
    Toward Heaven's sea of stars ;
Behind there was a wake of billows tossing,

        Before a glory lay.
O happy soul ! with all sail set, just crossing
        Into the Far-away ;
The gloom and gleam, the calmness and the
            strife,
Were death before thee, and behind thee life.

And as that ship went up the waters stately,
        Upon her topmasts tall
I saw two sails, whereof the one was greatly
        Dark, as a funeral pall.
But oh ! the next's pure whiteness who shall
            utter ?
        Like a shell-snowy strand,
Or when a sunbeam falleth through the shutter
        On a dead baby's hand ;
But both alike across the surging sea
Helped to the haven where the bark would be.

And as that soul went onward, sweetly speeding
        Unto its home and light,
Repentance made it sorrowful exceeding,
        Faith made it wondrous bright ;
Repentance dark with shadowy recollections,
        And longings unsufficed,

Faith white and pure with sunniest affections
    Full from the face of Christ:
But both across the sun-besilvered tide
Helped to the haven where the heart would ride.

BELIEVERS NOT SEEING.

E were not with the faithful few
   Who stood Thy bitter cross around,
Nor heard Thy prayer for those that
      slew,
Nor felt that earthquake rock the ground ;
We saw no spear-wound pierce Thy side :
Yet we believe that Thou hast died.

No angel's message met our ear
   On that first glorious Easter day, —
. " The Lord is risen, He is not here :
   Come, see the place where Jesus lay ! "
But we believe that Thou didst quell
The banded powers of death and hell.

We saw Thee not return on high ;
   And now, our longing sight to bless,
No ray of glory from the sky
   Shines down upon our wilderness :
Yet we believe that Thou art there,
And seek Thee, Lord, in praise and prayer.

"I KNOW IN WHOM I HAVE BELIEVED."

FROM tangled ways by which I wan-
    dered far
    In realms of doubt unlit of moon or star,
Where muttering fears and legioned phantoms
    are,
        Jesus, I come.

'T is not that I have found Thy temple's base,
Or yet among the clouds its top can trace,
Enough, henceforth I see its inner grace,
        Enough for me.

How rolls Thy Jordan to the wondrous sea
Of boundless Godhead still is hid from me,
I have such need to be baptized of Thee,
        Dear Christ, I come !

I see Thy white feet on Judea's hills,
I hear the melting flow of Kedron's rills,
Time's dreary desert all that vision fills,
        I know not how.

The ages show their garnered sheaves of thought,
By all the gleaning generations brought,
Some secret mildew on them all hath wrought,
            No food is there.

But in an upper room in Palestine
Is one that giveth mystic bread and wine,
I reach out for that nourishment divine,
            And faint no more.

Oh, many hands tear down Thy fane to-day,
Yet lo ! its stones all man's true building stay ;
Give unto me the gold without the clay,
            Oh, great High Priest. .

The marvels of Thy beauty draws me so,
The sweetness of Thy sacrificial woe,
Divinest vision that the world can show,
            Stay in my sight !

Though Reason close this way her sullen door,
Her scornful bolts shall baffle me no more,
Faith hath her secret wings by which to soar ;
            Faith bear me in !

"SEEK YE MY FACE—THY FACE, LORD, WILL I SEEK."

THROUGH my life, Thy spirit striving
  From Thy holy place,—
  Wandering, I have heard Thy guiding,—
" Child, seek ye my face."
Wandering after earthly treasure,
  I have turned away ;
Meanwhile, Thou my steps didst measure,
  Lest too far I 'd stray.
And when at some idol's splendor
  I have laid my trust,
Thou hast, with a care so tender,
  Trodden it to dust.

Low beside some fountain streaming
  I have knelt to drink,
There to quench my thirsty dreaming
  At its luring brink ;
Thou didst trouble, then, the waters,
  Till I turn'd aside,
And I knew it was an angel
  Touch'd its failing tide.

Now the living Fountain given
   Rises in its place,
And I rise from earth to heaven,
   Seeking, Lord, Thy face!

High Thy altar-fire is burning;
   There my lamp I light;
And my soul, from " strange fire " turning,
   Bows with veiled sight.
Far behind me, o'er life's mountains,
   Fade my tents in night —
Pilgrim from the wasted fountains —
   Follower after Light —
Trembler for Thy love immortal —
   Listener, till Thou speak —
Worshipper, " Seek ye my face,"
   " Thy face, Lord, will I seek."

STRENGTH IN WEAKNESS.

FATHER! for Thy kindest word
   Thankful songs to Thee I sing ;
   Sick at heart with hope deferred,
  All my cause to Thee I bring.
Sweet the sound I hear from Thee, —
Cast thy burden upon Me.

As a father, bending low,
  Listens to his lisping child,
So to me Thy pity show,
  By the world and sin beguiled.
Holy is Thy law, and just ;
Yet remember I am dust.

Spare me, Thou who lov'st to spare !
  Gently on me lay Thy hand !
Grasp the bruisèd reed with care !
  Let the smoking flax be fanned ;

Firm my faltering steps uphold ;
Tried, let me come forth like gold.

Oh remember Him who died,
  With His life my soul to save ;
Let me clasp the Crucified,
  Till I reach the awful grave ;
Then, the light affliction o'er,
Heaven is mine forevermore !

I SAID.

WHEN apple-blossoms in the spring
   Began their fragrant leaves to shed,
   And robins twittered on the wing,
" 'T is time to sow my seeds," I said.

So, patiently, with care and pains,
   My nurslings under-ground I spread.
" The early and the latter rains
   Will reach them where they lie," I said.

" The sun will nurse them, and the dew ;
   The sweet winds woo them overhead.
No care of mine shall coax them through
   This black, unsightly mould," I said.

And so I left them ; day by day,
   To gentle household duties wed,
I went in quiet on my way :
   " God will take care of them," I said.

And now 't is autumn ; rich and bright
   My garden blooms, — blue, white, and red ;

A loyal show! a regal sight!
  And all is even as I said.

My faithless heart! the lesson heed;
  No longer walk disquieted; —
Where the Great Sower·sows the seed,
  All shall be even as He said.

'T is spring-time yet; behold, the years
  Roll grandly in, God overhead,
When Thou shalt say, " Oh, bootless fears!
  Lo! all is even as He said."

THE COMPASS.

THOU art, O God, my East!   In Thee
  I dawned :
    Within me ever let Thy day-spring
      shine !
Then for each night of sorrow I have mourned,
  I 'll bless Thee, Father, since it seals me
    Thine.

Thou art, O God, my North !   My trembling
    soul,
  Like a charmed needle, points to Thee alone;
Each wave of time, each storm of life, shall roll
  My trusting spirit forward to Thy throne.

Thou art, O God, my South ! Thy fervent love
  Perennial verdure o'er my life hath shed,
And constant sunshine from Thy heart of love,
  With wine and oil Thy grateful child hath fed.

Thou art, O God, my West!   Into Thy arms,
  Glad as the setting sun, may I decline ;
Baptized from earthly storms and sin's alarms,
  Re-born, arise in Thy new heavens to shine.

MONT BLANC REVISITED.

 MOUNT beloved ! mine eyes again
Behold the twilight's sanguine strain
    Along thy peaks expire ;
O Mount beloved ! thy frontier waste
I seek with a religious haste
    And reverent desire.

They greet me midst thy shadows cold,
Such thoughts as holy men of old
    Amidst the desert found —
Such gladness as in Him they felt
Who with them through the darkness dwelt,
    And compass'd all around.

Oh, happy ! if His will were so,
To give me manna here for snow,
    And by the torrent-side
To lead me as He leads His flocks
Of wild deer, through the lonely rocks,
    In peace, unterrified.

Since, from the things that trustful rest, —
The partridge, on her purple nest,
      The marmot in his den, —
God wins a worship more resign'd —
A purer praise than He can find
      Upon the lips of men, —

Alas for man ! who hath no sense
Of gratefulness or confidence,
      But still rejects and raves ;
That all God's love can hardly win
One soul from taking pride in sin,
      And pleasure over graves.

Yet let me not, like him who trod
In wrath, of old, the Mount of God,
      Forget the thousands left,
Lest, haply, when I seek His face,
The whirlwind of the cave replace
      The glory of the cleft.

And teach me, God, a milder thought,
Lest I, of all Thy blood has bought,
      Least honorable be ;
And this that moves me to condemn
Be rather want of love for them
      Than jealousy for Thee.

And in Jesus Christ, His only Son, our Lord.

MY SHEEP HEAR MY VOICE.

DARKER than night, life's shadows fall
   around us,
   And, like benighted men, we miss our
   mark ;
God hides Himself, and grace hath scarcely
   found us,
   Ere Death finds out his victims in the dark !

Onward we go, for still we hear them singing,
   Come, weary souls ! for Jesus bids you come !
And through the dark, its echoes sweetly ringing,
   The music of the Gospel leads us home.

Far, far away, like bells at evening pealing,
   The voice of Jesus sounds o'er land and sea,
And laden souls, by thousands meekly stealing,
   Kind Shepherd ! turn their weary steps to
   Thee.

Cheer up, my soul! faith's moonbeams softly
   glisten
  Upon the breast of life's most troubled sea;
And it will cheer thy drooping heart to listen
  To those brave songs which angels mean for
   thee.

Angels! sing on, your faithful watches keeping,
  Sing us sweet fragments of the songs above;
While we toil on, and soothe ourselves with
   weeping,
  Till life's long night shall break in endless
   love.

THE SHADOW OF A GREAT ROCK IN A WEARY LAND.

THE rocky path still climbs the glowing
        steep
    Of Olivet ;
Though rains of two millenniums wear it deep,
    Men tread it yet.

Still to the gardens o'er the brook it leads,
        Quiet and low ;
Before his sheep the shepherd on it treads,
        His voice they know.

The wild fig throws broad shadows o'er it still,
        As once o'er Thee ;
Peasants go home at evening up that hill
        To Bethany.

And as when gazing Thou didst weep o'er
        them
        From height to height,
The white roofs of discrowned Jerusalem
        Burst on our sight.

These ways were strewed with garments once
and palm,
Which we tread thus ;
Here through Thy triumph on Thou passedst,
calm,
On to Thy Cross.

The waves have washt fresh sand upon the
shore
Of Galilee ;
But chiselled on the hill-sides evermore,
Thy paths we see.

Man has not changed them in that slumbering
land,
Nor time effaced :
Where Thy feet trod to bless we still may
stand ;
All can be traced.

Yet we have traces of Thy footsteps far
Truer than these ;
Where'er the poor and tried and suffering are,
Thy steps faith sees.

Nor with fond, sad regrets Thy steps we trace ;
Thou art not dead !

Our path is onward till we see Thy face
    And hear Thy tread.

And now wherever meets Thy lowliest band
    In praise and prayer,
There is Thy presence, there Thy Holy Land,—
    Thou, Thou art there !

THIS IS MY BELOVED AND THIS IS MY FRIEND.

JESUS, Thou Joy of loving hearts!
    Thou Fount of Life! Thou Light
      of men !
From the best bliss that earth imparts,
    We turn unfilled to Thee again.

Thy truth unchanged hath ever stood ;
    Thou savest those that on Thee call ;
To them that seek Thee, Thou art good,
    To them that find Thee — All in All !

We taste Thee, O Thou Living Bread,
    And long to feast upon Thee still ;
We drink of Thee, the Fountain Head,
    And thirst our souls from Thee to fill.

Our restless spirits yearn for Thee,
    Where'er our changeful lot is cast ;
Glad, when Thy gracious smile we see,
    Blest, when our faith can hold Thee fast.

O Jesu, ever with us stay!
　　Make all our moments calm and bright;
Chase the dark night of sin away, —
　　Shed o'er the world Thy holy light!

O LORD, THOU KNOWEST!

THOU knowest, Lord, the weariness
    and sorrow
  Of the sad heart that comes to Thee
    for rest.
Cares of to-day, and burdens for to-morrow,
  Blessings implored, and sins to be confest,—
I come before Thee at Thy gracious word,
And lay them at Thy feet—Thou knowest,
    Lord.

Thou knowest all the past,—how long and
    blindly
  On the dark mountains the lost wanderer
    strayed,—
How the Good Shepherd followed, and how
    kindly
  He bore it home, upon His shoulders laid,
And healed the bleeding wounds, and soothed
    the pain,
And brought back life, and hope, and strength
    again.

Thou knowest all the present, — each tempta-
 tion,
  Each toilsome duty, each foreboding fear ;
All to myself assigned of tribulation,
  Or to beloved ones, than self more dear !
All pensive memories, as I journey on,
Longings for vanished smiles, and voices gone !

Thou knowest all the future, — gleams of glad-
 ness,
  By stormy clouds too quickly overcast, —
Hours of sweet fellowship, and parting sadness,
  And the dark river to be crossed at last : —
Oh, what could confidence and hope afford
To tread that path, but this, — *Thou knowest,*
 Lord!

Thou knowest, not alone as God, all-know-
 ing, —
  As *man* our mortal weakness Thou hast
  proved ;
On earth, with purest sympathies o'erflowing,
 Oh, Saviour ! Thou hast wept, and Thou
  hast loved !
And love and sorrow still to Thee may come,
And find a hiding place, a rest, a home.

Therefore I come, Thy gentle call obeying,
  And lay my sins and sorrows at Thy feet,
On everlasting strength my weakness staying,
  Clothed in Thy robe of righteousness com-
    plete :
Then rising and refreshed, I leave Thy throne,
And follow on to know as I am known !

RABBI, WHERE DWELLEST THOU ? —
COME AND SEE.

MASTER, where abidest Thou ?
  Lamb of God, 't is Thee we seek,
  For the wants which press us now
Other aid is all too weak.
Canst Thou take our sins away ?
  May we find repose in Thee ?
From the gracious lips to-day,
  As of old, breathes, " Come and see."

Master, where abidest Thou ?
  We would leave the past behind ;
We would scale the mountain's brow,
  Learning more Thy heavenly mind.
Still a look is all our lore,
  The transforming look to Thee ;
From the living Truth once more
  Breathes the answer, " Come and see."

Master, where abidest Thou ?
  How shall we Thine image best

Bear in light upon our brow,
   Stamp in love upon our breast ?
Still a look is all our might :
   Looking draws the heart to Thee,
Sends us from the absorbing sight
   With the message, " Come and see."

Master, where abidest Thou ?
   All the springs of life are low ;
Sin and grief our spirits bow,
   And we wait Thy call to go.
From the depths of happy rest,
   Where the just abide with Thee :
From the Voice which makes them blest,
   Comes the summons, " Come and see."

Christian ! tell it to thy brother,
   From life's dawning till its end ;
Every hand may clasp another,
   And the loneliest bring a friend ;
Till the veil is drawn aside,
   And from where her home shall be,
Bursts upon the enfranchised Bride
   The triumphant " Come and see."

THE WELL AT SYCHAR.

THEY have stopped the sacred well
    which the Patriarchs dug of old,
Where they watered the patient flocks
    at noon, from the depths so pure and
    cold ;
Where the Saviour asked for drink, and found
    at noon repose :
But the living spring He opened then no human
    hands can close.

They have scattered the ancient stones, where
    at noon He sat to rest :
None ever shall rest by that well again, and
    think how His accents blessed :
But the Rest for the burdened heart, the Shade
    in the weary land,
The riven Rock, with its living streams, forever
    unmoved shall stand.

Earth has no Temple now, no beautiful House
    of God,

Or earth is all one temple-floor, which those
    sacred feet have trod.
But in Heaven there is a Throne, a Home, and
    a House of Prayer;
Thyself the Temple; Thyself the Sun. Our
    pilgrimage endeth there!

COME, BLESSED JESU.

THE Galilean fishers toil
    All night, and nothing take ;
    But Jesus comes, — a wondrous spoil
Is lifted from the lake.

Lord, when our labors are in vain,
    And vain the help of men,
When fruitless is the care and pain,
    Come, blessed Jesu, then !

The night is dark, the surges fill
    The bark, the wild winds roar ;
But Jesus comes ; and all is still, —
    The ship is at the shore.

O Lord, when storms around us howl,
    And all is dark and drear,
In all the tempests of the soul,
    O blessed Jesu, hear !

A frail one thrice denying Thee
    Saw mercy in Thine eyes ;

The penitent upon the tree
  Was borne to Paradise.

In hours of sin and deep distress
  O show us, Lord, Thy face ;
In penitential loneliness,
  O give us, Jesu, grace !

The faithful few retire in fear
  To their closed upper-room ;
But suddenly, with joyful cheer,
  They see their Master come.

Lord, come to us, unloose our bands,
  And bid our terrors cease,
Lift over us Thy blessed hands,
  Speak, holy Jesu, Peace.

In days when Faith will scarce be found,
  And wolves be in the fold,
When sin and sorrow will abound,
  And Charity wax cold,

Then hear Thy Saints, who to Thee pray
  To bring them to their home ;
Hear, when the Bride and Spirit say,
  " Come, blessed Jesu, come ! "

THE LOVE OF CHRIST WHICH PASSETH KNOWLEDGE.

I BORE with thee long weary days and
              nights,
    Through many pangs of heart, through
        many tears ;
I bore with thee, thy hardness, coldness, slights,
    For three and thirty years.

Who else had dared for thee what I have dared?
    I plunged the depth most deep from bliss
        above ;
I not My flesh, I not My spirit spared :
    Give thou Me love for love.

For thee I thirsted in the daily drouth,
    For thee I trembled in the nightly frost :
Much sweeter thou than honey to My mouth :
    Why wilt thou still be lost ?

I bore thee on My shoulders and rejoiced :
    Men only marked upon My shoulders borne

The branding cross; and shouted hungry-
    voiced,
  Or wagged their heads in scorn.

Thee did nails grave upon My hands, thy name
  Did thorns for frontlets stamp between Mine
    eyes :
I Holy ONE, put on thy guilt and shame,
    I, GOD, Priest, Sacrifice.

A thief upon My right hand and My left;
  Six hours alone, athirst, in misery :
At length in death one smote My heart, and
    cleft
    A hiding-place for thee.

Nailed to the racking cross, than bed of down
  More dear, whereon to stretch Myself and
    sleep :
So did I win a kingdom — share My crown;
    A harvest — come and reap.

FOR US ALSO.

JESU! behold, the Wise from far,
Led to Thy cradle by a star,
Bring gifts to Thee, their God
and King!
O guide us by Thy light, that we
The way may find, and still to Thee
Our hearts, our all, for tribute bring!

Jesu! the pure, the spotless Lamb,
Who to the Temple humbly came,
Duteous, the legal rites to pay!
O make our proud, our stubborn will
All Thy wise, gracious laws fulfil,
Whate'er rebellious nature say!

Jesu! who on the fatal wood
Pour'dst out Thy life's last drop of blood,
Nailed to the accursed shameful cross!
O may we bless Thy love, and be
Ready, dear Lord, to bear for Thee
All shame, all grief, all pain, and loss!

Jesu! who by Thine own love slain,
By Thine own power took'st life again,
  And Conqueror from the grave didst rise!
O may Thy death our souls revive,
And ev'n on earth a new life give,
  A glorious life, that never dies!

Jesu! who to Thy heaven again
Return'dst in triumph, there to reign,
  Of men and angels sovereign King!
O may our parting souls take flight
Up to that land of joy and light,
  And there forever grateful sing!

All glory to the sacred Three,
One undivided Deity!
  All honor, power, and love, and praise!
Still may Thy blessed Name shine bright
In beams of uncreated light,
  Crowned with its own eternal rays!

THE ISRAELITES AT THE RED SEA.

BEHIND them lies the desert waste ;
　　Before, the pathless deep ;
　　And on their track with vengeful haste
Egypt's dark squadrons sweep ;
Till in the sunset's last red glow
Flashes the armor of the foe !

Then rose to Heaven a mighty cry ;
　　A people's voice was on the air, —
In every heart, in every eye,
　　Rebellion and despair :
" Why didst thou thus our steps beguile ?
Were there no graves beside the Nile ?

" Where are the pleasant things and fair
　　That grow by Egypt's streams ?
Is this lone waste, the lion's lair,
　　The Canaan of our dreams ? —
This dark blue sea, this barren strand,
The pathway to the Promised Land ? "

The word is spoken ! — o'er the wave
　　Is stretched the leader's mystic rod ;

And safely, through the yawning grave
  Where human foot had never trod,
They reach at dawn the distant shore, —
Their buried foes are seen no more.

O Lord, when, like Thy sons of old,
  We wander through a barren waste,
Where Hope is faint and Love is cold,
  And bitter to our earthly taste
The stream that in the desert flows,
The daily bread Thy hand bestows, —

When haunting dreams of pleasant things
  Make the lone wilderness more drear,
Where every hour in passing brings
  Some present pain, some threatening fear,
And stretched before our shrinking eyes,
Like a dark sea, the future lies, —

Then, Lord, be Thou at hand to guide,
  Thy Cross be there our path to mark :
Though high may swell the stormy tide,
  In Heaven is light, though earth be dark.
Like those who crossed that Eastern sea,
We *shall* be safe who trust in Thee !

THE WAY OF SORROWS.

O LORD, the wilderness to me
 A very Paradise shall be,
 Since Thou for forty days wast there,
In fasting, solitude, and prayer !

Unworthy though these feet to rest
On ground Thy footsteps once have blest,
The way of sorrows shall be mine,
Made sweet because it first was Thine.

Lord, let me find some lowly place
Where I may seek Thy pitying face,
And plead with Thee by Olivet,
By agony, and bloody sweat.

Some quiet aisle or dim recess
Shall make for me a wilderness ;
And surely Angels shall be there
To wait on penitence and prayer.

Nor is this all : for I would know
The depth of shame, the crown of woe,
Stand by the stricken Mother's side,
While Thou art mocked and crucified.

And then in hours of saddest gloom
I still will watch around Thy tomb,
Till with the day new joy be born,
And Thou shalt rise on Easter-morn.

Oh, blessed thought, that faith can see
In every altar — Calvary,
Find there the loving arms outspread,
And fall before the fallen Head.

Come King of kings, come Light of light :
The Bride awaits the day all bright,
When she shall lift, her mourning o'er,
The shout of Paschal joy once more.

EMMAUS.

THEY talked of Jesus, as they went ;
  And Jesus, all unknown,
  Did at their side himself present
With sweetness all His own.
Swift, as He oped the sacred word,
  His glory they discerned ;
And swift, as His dear voice they heard,
  Their hearts within them burned.

He would have left them, but that they
  With prayers His love assailed :
" Depart not yet ! a little stay ! "
  They pressed Him, and prevailed.
And Jesus was revealed, as there
  He blessed and brake the bread :
But, while they marked His heavenly air,
  The matchless Guest had fled.

And thus at times, as Christians talk
  Of Jesus and His word,
He joins two friends amidst their walk,
  And makes, unseen, a third.

And oh ! how sweet their converse flows,
   Their holy theme how clear,
How warm with love each bosom glows,
   If Jesus be but near !

And they that woo His visits sweet,
   And will not let Him go,
Oft, while His broken bread they eat,
   His soul-felt presence know :
His gathered friends He loves to meet
   And fill with joy their faith,
When they with melting hearts repeat
   The memory of His death.

But such sweet visits here are brief;
   Dispensed from stage to stage,
(A cheering and a prized relief,)
   Of faith's hard pilgrimage.
'There is a scene where Jesus ne'er,
   Ne'er leaves His happy guests ;
He spreads a ceaseless banquet there,
   And love still fires their breasts.

SUNDAY EVE.

O TIME of tranquil joy and holy feeling!
When over earth God's spirit from
above
  Spreads out His wings of love!
When sacred thoughts, like angels, come ap-
pealing
To our tent-doors; O eve, to earth and heaven
  The sweetest of the seven!

How peaceful are thy skies! thy air is clearer,
As on the advent of a gracious time:
  The sweetness of its prime
Blesseth the world, and Eden's days seem nearer:
I hear, in each faint stirring of the breeze,
  God's voice among the trees.

O while thy hallowed moments are distilling
Their fresher influence on my heart like dews,
  The chamber where I muse
Turns to a temple! He, whose converse thrilling
Honored Emmaus, that old eventide,
  Comes sudden to my side.

'T is light at evening time when Thou art pres-
       ent;
Thy coming to the eleven in that dim room
    Brightened, O Christ! its gloom:
So bless my lonely hour that memories pleasant
Around the time a heavenly gleam may cast,
    Which many days shall last!

Raise each low aim, refine each high emotion,
That with more ardent footstep I may press
    Toward Thy holiness;
And, braced for sacred duty by devotion,
Support my cross along that rugged road
    Which Thou hast sometime trod!

I long to see Thee, for my heart is weary:
O when, my Lord! in kindness wilt Thou come
    To call Thy banished home?
The scenes are cheerless, and the days are
       dreary;
From sorrow and from sin I would be free,
    And evermore with Thee!

AT THE DOOR.

BEHOLD! a Stranger's at the door!
He gently knocks, has knocked before,
Has waited long, is waiting still;
You treat no other friend so ill.

But will He prove a Friend indeed?
He will! the very Friend you need!
The Man of Nazareth, 't is He,
With garments dyed at Calvary.

Rise, touched with gratitude Divine;
Turn out His enemy and thine,
That hateful, hell-born monster, sin;
And let the Heavenly Stranger in.

If thou art poor, (and poor thou art,)
Lo! He has riches to impart;
Not wealth, in which mean avarice rolls;
O better far! the wealth of souls!

Thou 'rt blind ; He 'll take the scales away,
And let in everlasting day :
Naked thou art ; but He shall dress
Thy blushing soul in righteousness.

Admit Him, for the human breast
Ne'er entertained so kind a guest :
Admit Him, for you can't expel ;
Where'er He comes, He comes to dwell.

Admit Him, ere His anger burn ;
His feet, departed, ne'er return !
Admit Him ; or the hour 's at hand
When at His door denied you 'll stand.

Yet know, (nor of the terms complain,)
If Jesus comes, He comes to reign ;
To reign, and with no partial sway ;
Thoughts must be slain, that disobey !

Sovereign of souls !   Thou Prince of Peace !
O may Thy gentle reign increase !
Throw wide the door, each willing mind !
And be His empire all mankind !

HYMN FOR EPIPHANY.

THE wise men to Thy cradle throne,
 O Infant Saviour, brought of old
The incense meet for God alone,
Sharp myrrh, and shining gold.

Shine on us too, sweet Eastern star,
 Thine own baptizèd Gentile band,
Till we have found our Lord from far,
 An offering in our hand.

Till we have brought the fine gold rare,
 Of zeal that giveth all for love ;
Till we have prayed the glowing prayer,
 Like incense borne above.

Till bitter tears our eyes have wet,
 Because our wilful hearts would err ;
Worship, and love, and sorrow met,
 Gold, frankincense, and myrrh.

All meet for Thee our own Adored,
 Our suffering Saviour, God, and King ;
Accept the gold and incense, Lord,
 Accept the myrrh we bring.

REST

REST, weary heart,
    From all thy silent griefs, and secret
        pain,
Thy profitless regrets, and longings vain ;
Wisdom and love have ordered all the past,
All shall be blessedness and light at last ;
Cast off the cares that have so long opprest ;
    Rest, sweetly rest !

    Rest, weary head !
Lie down to slumber in the peaceful tomb :
Light from above has broken through its gloom ;
Here, in the place where once thy Saviour lay,
Where He shall wake thee on a future day,
Like a tired child upon its mother's breast,
    Rest, sweetly rest !

    Rest, spirit free !
In the green pastures of the heavenly shore,
Where sin and sorrow can approach no more,

With all the flock by the Good Shepherd fed,
Beside the streams of Life eternal led,
Forever with thy God and Saviour blest,
Rest, sweetly rest !

"I AM THINE."

THAT I am Thine, my Lord and God !
Sprinkled and ransom'd by Thy blood,—
   Repeat that word once more,
With such an energy and light,
That this world's flattery or spite
   To shake me never may have power.

From various cares my heart retires ;
Though deep and boundless its desires,
   I 'm now to please but One :
He, before whom the elders bow,
With Him is all my business now,
   And with the souls that are His own.

This is my joy, (which ne'er can fail,)
To see my Saviour's arm prevail ;
   To mark the steps of grace ;
How new-born souls, convinced of sin,
His blood reveal'd to them within,
   Extol my Lord in every place.

With these my happy lot is cast:
Through the world's deserts, rude and waste,
Or through its gardens fair;
Whether the storm of malice sweeps,
Or all in dead supineness sleeps;
    Still to go on be my whole care.

See! the dear flock by Jesus drawn,
In blest simplicity move on;
    They trust His shepherd's crook.
Beholders many faults will find,
But they can tell their Saviour's mind;
    Content, if written in His Book.

No, my dear Lord, in following Thee,
Not in the dark uncertainly,
    This foot obedient moves:
'T is with a brother and a King,
Who many to His yoke will bring;
    Who ever lives and ever loves.

Now then, my Way, my Truth, my Life!
Henceforth let sorrow, doubt, and strife
    Drop off, like autumn leaves; —
Henceforth, as privileged by Thee,
Simple and undistracted be
    My soul, which to Thy sceptre cleaves.

JESUS IS GOD!

JESUS is God! the glorious bands
   Of golden angels sing
   Songs of adoring praise to Him,
  Their Maker and their King.
He was true God in Bethlehem's crib,
   On Calvary's cross true God,
He who in Heaven eternal reigned,
   In time on earth abode.

Jesus is God! there never was
   A time when He was not :
Boundless, eternal, merciful,
   The Word the Sire begot!
Backward our thoughts through ages stretch,
   Onward through endless bliss, —
For there are two eternities,
   And both alike are His !

Jesus is God! let sorrow come,
   And pain, and every ill ;

All are worth while, for all are means
 His glory to fulfil ;   ·
Worth while a thousand years of life
 To speak one little word,
If by our Credo we might own
 The Godhead of our Lord !

Jesus is God ! O could I now
 But ·compass land and sea,
To teach and tell this single truth,
 How happy should I be !
O had I but an angel's voice,
 I would proclaim so loud,
Jesus, the good, the beautiful,
 Is everlasting God !

Jesus is God ! If on the earth
 This blessed faith decays,
More tender must our love become,
 More plentiful our praise.
We are not angels, but we may
 Down in earth's corners kneel,
And multiply sweet acts of love,
 And murmur what we feel.

WORTHY THE LAMB.

HERE on earth, where foes surround us,
　　While our trembling souls within
　　Feel the fetters which have bound us,
　Feel the burden of our sin ;
Lord, on Thee alone relying,
　Strength we crave to burst our chain,
Ever pleading, ever crying,
　" Lord, for us the Lamb was slain."

In those high and holy regions
　Where the blest Thy praise prolong,
Cherubs and seraphic legions
　Know no theme of nobler song ;
White-robed saints, who there adore Thee
　Throned above the glassy main,
Sing, and cast their crowns before Thee,
　" Lord, for us the Lamb was slain."

Thus Thy Church, whate'er her dwelling,
　Heaven above or earth below,
One harmonious chorus swelling,
　Loves her Saviour's praise to show :
Here in trial, there in glory,
　Changeless rings the immortal strain,
Changeless sounds the wondrous story,
　" Lord, for us the Lamb was slain."

I WILL NOT LET THEE GO.

COME, O Thou Traveller unknown,
  Whom still I hold, but cannot see !
  My company before is gone,
And I am left alone with Thee ;
With Thee all night I mean to stay,
And wrestle till the break of day.

I need not tell Thee who I am ;
  My misery and sin declare ;
Thyself hast call'd me by my name ;
  Look on Thy hands and read it there :
But who, I ask Thee, who art Thou ?
Tell me Thy name, and tell me now.

In vain Thou strugglest to get free,
  I never will unloose my hold :
Art Thou the Man that died for me ?
  The secret of Thy love unfold :
Wrestling, I will not let Thee go.
Till I Thy name, Thy nature know.

Wilt Thou not yet to me reveal
 Thy new, unutterable name ?
Tell me, I still beseech Thee, tell ?
 To know it now, resolved I am :
Wrestling, I will not let Thee go :
Till I Thy name, Thy nature know.

My prayer hath power with God : the grace
 Unspeakable I now receive ;
Through faith I see Thee face to face ;
 I see Thee face to face, and live !
In vain I have not wept and strove ;
Thy nature and Thy name is Love.

I know Thee, Saviour, who Thou art,
 Jesus, the feeble sinner's friend :
Nor wilt Thou with the night depart,
 But stay, and love me to the end :
Thy mercies never shall remove ;
Thy nature and Thy name is Love.

The Sun of Righteousness on me
 Hath risen, with healing in His wings ;
Wither'd my nature's strength, from Thee
 My soul its life and succor brings ;
My help is all laid up above ;
Thy nature and Thy name is Love.

THE BOY WITH THE FIVE LOAVES.

WHAT time the Saviour spread His feast
　　For thousands on the mountain's side,
One of the last and least
The abundant store supplied.

Haply, the wonders to behold,
　　A boy 'mid other boys he came,
A lamb of Jesus' fold,
　　Though now unknown by name.

Or for his sweet obedient ways
　　The Apostles brought him near, to share
Their Lord's laborious days,
　　His frugal basket bear.

Or might it be, his duteous heart,
　　That led him sacrifice to bring
For his own simple part,
　　To the world's hidden King ?

Well may I guess how glow'd his cheek,
 How he look'd down, half pride, half fear ;
Far off he saw one speak
 Of him, in Jesus' ear.

" There is a lad, — five loaves hath he,
 And fishes twain ; but what are they
Where hungry thousands be ? "
 Nay, Christ will find a way.

In order, on the fresh green hill,
 The mighty Shepherd ranks His sheep,
By tens and fifties, still
 As clouds when breezes sleep.

Oh, who can tell the trembling joy,
 Who paint the grave, endearing look,
When from that favored boy
 The wondrous pledge He took ?

Keep thou, dear child, thine early word ;
 Bring Him thy best : who knows but He,
For his eternal board,
 May take some gift of thee ?

Thou prayest without the veil as yet ;
 But kneel in faith ; an arm benign

Such prayers will duly set
  Within the holiest shrine.

And prayer has might to spread and grow ;
  Thy childish darts, right aim'd on high,
May catch Heaven's fire, and glow
  Far in the eternal sky !

Even as He made that stripling's store
  Type of the feast by Him decreed,
Where angels might adore,
  And souls forever feed.

CHRIST AND THE LITTLE ONES.

"THE Master has come over Jordan,"
    Said Hannah, the mother, one day ;
    "Is healing the people who throng Him
With a touch of His finger, they say.

"And now I shall carry the children, —
    Little Rachel, and Samuel, and John ;
I shall carry the baby, Esther,
    For the Lord to look upon."

The father looked at her kindly,
    But he shook his head and smiled :
"Now who but a doting mother
    Would think of a thing so wild !

"If the children were tortured by demons,
    Or dying of fever, — 't were well, —
Or had they the taint of the leper,
    Like many in Israel."

" Nay, do not hinder me, Nathan,
　　I feel such a burden of care, —
If I carry it to the Master
　　Perhaps I shall leave it there.

" If He lay His hand on the children,
　　My heart will be lighter I know,
For a blessing for ever and ever
　　Will follow them as they go."

So over the hills of Judah,
　　Along by the vine-rows green,
With Esther asleep on her bosom,
　　And Rachel her brothers between ;

'Mong the people who hung on His teaching,
　　Or waited His touch and His word,
Through the row of proud Pharisees listening,
　　She pressed to the feet of the Lord.

" Now why shouldst thou hinder the Master,"
　　Said Peter, " with children like these ?
Seest not how from morning till evening
　　He teacheth, and healeth disease ? "

Then Christ said : " Forbid not the children,
　　Permit them to come unto me ;"

And He took in His arms little Esther,
  And Rachel He set on His knee;

And the heavy heart of the mother
  Was lifted all earth-care above,
As He laid His hands on the brothers,
  And blest them with tenderest love:

As He said of the babes in His bosom,
  "Of such are the kingdom of heaven;" —
And strength for all duty and trial,
  That hour to her spirit was given.

"MY MEDITATION OF HIM SHALL BE SWEET."

WHEN languor and disease invade
  This trembling house of clay,
  'T is sweet to look beyond our cage,
And long to soar away.

Sweet to look inward, and attend
  The whispers of His love ;
Sweet to look upward to the throne,
  Where Jesus pleads above.

Sweet to look back, and see my name
  In life's fair book mark'd down ;
Sweet to look forward, and behold
  Eternal joys my own.

Sweet to reflect how grace divine
  My sins on Jesus laid ;
Sweet to remember that His blood
  My debt of suffering paid.

Sweet in His righteousness to stand,
  Which saves from second death ;
Sweet to experience, day by day,
  His Spirit's quickening breath.

Sweet on His faithfulness to rest,
  Whose love can never end ;
Sweet on His covenant of grace
  For all things to depend.

Sweet in the confidence of faith
  To trust His firm decrees ;
Sweet to lie passive in His hand,
  And have no will but His.

Sweet to rejoice in lively hope
  That when my change shall come,
Angels will hover round my bed,
  And waft my spirit home.

There shall my dis-imprison'd soul
  Behold Him and adore ;
Be with His likeness satisfied,
  And grieve and sin no more :

Shall see Him wear that very flesh
  On which my guilt was lain ;

His love intense, His merit fresh,
  As though but newly slain.

Soon, too, my slumbering dust shall hear
  The trumpet's quickening sound !
And by my Saviour's power rebuilt,
  At His right hand be found.

These eyes shall see Him in that day ;
  The God that died for me ;
And all my rising bones shall say,
  Lord, who is like to Thee !

If such the views which grace unfolds,
  Weak as it is below,
What raptures must the Church above,
  In Jesu's presence, know !

If such the sweetness of the stream,
  What must that fountain be,
Where saints and angels draw their bliss
  Immediately from Thee !

O may the unction of these truths
  Forever with me stay ;
Till from her sinful cage dismiss'd,
  My spirit flies away !

"CHRIST IN YOU, THE HOPE OF GLORY."

SUPREME High-Priest, the pilgrim's
    light,
  My heart for Thee prepare ;
Thine image stamp, and deeply write
  Thy superscription there :
Ah, let my forehead bear Thy seal,
  My arm Thy badge retain ;
My heart the inward witness feel
  That I am born again !

O that the penetrating sight
  And eagle's eye were mine !
Undazzled at the boundless light
  Of Majesty divine :
That with the armies of the sky
  I, too, may sit and sing,
Add, Saviour, to the eagle's eye,
  The dove's aspiring wing.

LOVE OF LOVE.

" *Many waters cannot quench love, neither can the
floods drown it ; if a man would give all the substance
of his house for love, it would utterly be contemned.*"
— CANT. viii. 7.

LOVE, in all its depth and height,
  I will sing, and never weary, —
    Love, which maketh life so bright,
  And the drooping heart so cheery, —
Love, whose fountain is with God,
  And whose streams, in Christ descending,
Flow where'er His footsteps trod,
  With all human blessings blending.

Love, in all its strength and might,
  I will sing, and I will prove it ;
Love eternal, infinite,
  Loveth me, and I will love it.
All I am, or hope to be,
  From that fount of life descending,
Riseth like a well in me,
  Ever fresh and never ending.

Sunbeams dancing on the sea,
    South wind blowing o'er the meadow,
Bird and blossom on the tree,
    Summer shine and summer shadow, —
Outward glancings of the Love
    That within, in fadeless beauty,
Lights and leads my steps above,
    Up the rugged paths of duty.

Love! my God and King Thou art!
    Ever will I bow before Thee;
Ever shall this grateful heart
    Own Thy kingdom and adore Thee;
Neither life nor death can e'er
    From Thy love, my Saviour, sever;
Love hath made the sinner dear,
    And that love endureth ever.

"COME UNTO ME."

ART thou weary ? art thou languid ?
  Art thou sore distrest ?
  "Come to Me," saith One, " and coming,
          Be at rest ! "

Hath He marks to lead me to Him,
  If He be my Guide ?
" In His feet and hands are wound-prints,
          And His side."

Is there diadem, as monarch,
  That His brow adorns ?
" Yea, a crown in very surety,
          But of thorns ! "

If I find Him, if I follow,
  What His guerdon here ?
" Many a sorrow, many a labor,
          Many a tear."

If I still hold closely to Him,
   What hath He at last ?
" Sorrow vanquish'd, labor ended,
          Jordan past ! "

If I ask Him to receive me,
   Will He say me nay ?
" Not till earth, and not till heaven
          Pass away ! "

Tending, following, keeping, struggling,
   Is He sure to bless ?
" Angels, martyrs, prophets, pilgrims,
          Answer, Yes."

A HYMN OF ANGELUS, OF THE SEVENTEENTH CENTURY.

O LOVE, who formedst me to wear
    The image of Thy Godhead here ;
    Who soughtest me with tender care
Through all my wanderings wild and drear ;
    O Love, I give myself to Thee,
    Thine ever, only Thine to be.

O Love, who ere life's earliest dawn
    Thy choice on me hath gently laid ;
O Love, who here as man wast born,
    And wholly like to us wast made ;
    O Love, I give myself to Thee,
    Thine ever, only Thine to be.

O Love, who once in time wast slain,
    Pierced through and through with bitter woe ;

O Love, who wrestling thus didst gain,
  That we eternal joy might know ;
    O Love, I give myself to Thee,
    Thine ever, only Thine to be.

O Love, of whom is truth and light,
  The Word and Spirit, life and power,
Whose heart was bared to them that smite,
  To shield us in our trial hour ;
    O Love, I give myself to Thee,
    Thine ever, only Thine to be.

O Love, who lovest me for aye,
  Who for my soul dost ever plead ;
O Love, who didst my ransom pay,
  Whose power sufficeth in my stead ;
    O Love, I give myself to Thee,
    Thine ever, only Thine to be.

O Love, who once shalt bid me rise
  From out this dying life of ours ;
O Love, who once o'er yonder skies
  Shall set me in the fadeless bowers ;
    O Love, I give myself to Thee,
    Thine ever, only Thine to be.

CHRIST ALL IN ALL.

SAY, art thou wounded, feeble, weak?
   In Jesus thy Physician seek;
   Does fever strike, or parching thirst?
He is thy Fountain, best and first;
Or, art thou bowed beneath sin's load?
He is thy Justice — fly to God;
Does soul or body sickness thrall?
He is the health of both, and all.

If thou wouldst fly the mists of night,
The Sun of Justice is thy light;
He bids the tongue-tied spirit speak,
Unties it in confession meek:
Or seek ye food? He gives thee bread;
Thou art by heavenly manna fed:
O hidden God, what harm can fall?
He gives Himself, He gives thee all.

JESUS PASSETH BY.

THOU passest by — Thy awful step I
　　hear ;
　　Thou passest by — thy five dread
　　wounds I see ;
Thou passest by — Thy saving cross I clasp
　With penitential tears of agony.

Thou passest by — I will not let Thee go
　Until Thy mercy streams into my soul ;
I am sin-laden ; lift the burden off,
　For Thou alone canst heal and make me
　　whole.

Renew my spirit with unswerving faith,
　While pondering on the path Thy saints
　　have trod ;
With hope and courage nerve this feeble frame
　To follow Thee, thou ever-present God.

Thou passest by — I pray to be illumed
  With grace and light ; so shall the darkness
     flee :
And these dim eyes, O Thou ascended Lord,
  In rapture recognize and gaze on Thee.

THE ANSWER.

THE merry world did, on a day,
　　With his trainbands and mates agree
　　To meet together where I lay,
And all in sport to jeer at me.

First, Beauty crept into a rose,
　　Which, when I plucked not, Sir, said she,
Tell me, I pray, whose hands are those?
　　But Thou shalt answer, Lord, for me.

Then Money came; and, chinking still,
　　What tune is this, poor man? said he;
I heard in music you had skill;
　　But Thou shalt answer, Lord, for me.

Then came brave Glory puffing by,
　　In silks that whistled, who but he?
He scarce allowed me half an eye;
　　But Thou shalt answer, Lord, for me.

Then came quick Wit and Conversation,
    And he would needs a comfort be ;
And, to be short, make an oration ;
    But Thou shalt answer, Lord, for me.

Yet when the hour of Thy design
    To answer these fine things shall come,
Speak not at large ; say, I am Thine ;
    And then they have their answer home.

CHRIST'S WORD, "ABIDE."

PERPETUAL peace flows from that
    word,
    A fountain by our Lord supplied ;
The 'twelve who followed Him, how oft they
    heard
    Their Teacher say, Abide !

It hangs — a bough of promises,
    Thick blossoming on every side ;
" I will not leave you comfortless," He says,
    " If ye in me Abide."

Lord, let my heart be wholly Thine ;
    I would not with the world divide ;
E'en as the branch abideth in the vine,
    Would I in thee Abide.

" Abide in me, and I in you."
    Would I to Thee were so allied !
Then would be one who now, alas ! are two :
    When shall I thus Abide ?

Near old Emmaus, had it been
  With me Thou walked'st at eventide,
Would I have asked Thee, as a stranger, in,
  Or said, " My Lord ! Abide ? "

Alas ! I too have walked with Thee —
  My whole way darkly by Thy side ;
I now invite Thee, Lord ! come in with me —
  Not tarry, but Abide !

Oh, Jesus ! make my dwelling Thine !
  Sit at my board, and there preside,
Till I can call Thy heavenly mansion mine,
  And there *Thy* guest Abide.

Yet lifted to Thy presence oft,
  Down — of my own weak faith — I glide.
Lend me again Thy wings to mount aloft,
  Then make me there Abide !

Come, oh, Lord Jesus ! quickly come !
  Why should I live, since Thou hast died ?
Earth is a cross, and life a martyrdom ;
  Let me with Thee Abide !

SUNDAY NEXT BEFORE ADVENT.

" Thou art fair, my love ; there is no spot in thee." —
CANT. iv. 7.

WOULD that I were fairer, Lord !
  More what Thy bride should be, —
  More meet to be the sharer, Lord,
Of love and heaven with Thee ;
Yet if Thy love with me Thou 'lt share,
I know that love can make me fair.

O would that I were purer, Lord !
  More filled with grace divine ! —
O would that I were surer, Lord,
  That my whole heart is Thine !
Were it so pure that I might see
Thy beauty, I would grow like Thee.

O would that I could higher, Lord,
  Above thees senses live !
Each feeling, each desire, my Lord,
  Could wholly to Thee give !
The love I thus would daily share,
That love alone would make me fair.

A DEATH-BED HYMN.

"WE would see Jesus;" for the shadows lengthen
    Across this little landscape of our life.
"We would see Jesus," our weak faith to strengthen
    For the last weariness — the final strife.

"We would see Jesus;" for life's hand hath rested,
    With its dark touch, upon both heart and brow,
And though our souls have many a billow breasted,
    Others are rising in the distance now.

"We would see Jesus," the great rock foundation,
    Whereon our feet were set by sovereign grace ;
Not life, nor death, with all their agitation,
    Shall thence remove us if we see His face.

"We would see Jesus." Other lights are
    paling,
Which for long years we have rejoiced to see ;
The blessings of our pilgrimage are failing ;
    We would not mourn them, for we go to
    Thee.

"We would see Jesus ; " yet the spirit lingers
    Round the dear object it has loved so long ;
And earth from earth can scarce unclose its
    fingers ;
    Our love to Thee makes not this love less
    strong.

"We would see Jesus." Sense is all too
    blinding,
And heaven appears too dim, too far away ;
We would see Thee, to gain a sweet reminding
    That Thou hast promised our great debt to
    pay.

"We would see Jesus ; " this is all we 're
    needing :
    Strength, joy, and willingness come with the
    sight ;
We would see Jesus, — dying, risen, pleading ;
    Then welcome day, and farewell mortal night.

THE THREE WONDERS.

THE wonder-working Master
　　Once deigned His race to save,
　When dry land for His people
　He made the Red Sea wave :
Now born for us, all willing,
　　Of maiden pure and sweet,
The path to heavenly mansions
　　He opens to our feet.

The bush unburned most truly
　　Portrays the holy womb,
Whence sprang the Word Incarnate
　　To loose the ancient doom,
And all the bitter sorrows
　　Of Eva's curse to stay,
The Word, who hither wended
　　Our sin to do away.

To Him, with God the Father
In substance truly one,
One with mankind, from all men
Be laud forever done :
God to our human nature,
To our mortality
In form conjoined, we worship,
And Him we glorify.

Thee, Word of God eternal,
Who wert before the sun,
The star showed to the Magi,
A poor and suffering One :
Thee, swaddled in a manger,
They saw with glad accord,
And hailed Thee with rejoicing,
True Man, and yet the Lord.

Born of the Virgin Mary.

COME! YE LOFTY, COME! YE LOWLY.

COME ! ye lofty, come ! ye lowly,
   Let your songs of gladness ring,
In a stable lies the Holy,
   In a manger rests the King :
See, in·Mary's arms reposing,
   Christ by highest heaven adored :
Come ! your circle round him closing,
   Pious hearts that love the Lord.

Come ! ye poor, no pomp of station
   Robes the Child your hearts adore :
He, the Lord of all salvation,
   Shares your want, is weak and poor :
Oxen, round about behold them,
   Rafters naked, cold, and bare,
See ! the shepherds, God has told them
   That the Prince of Life lies there.

Come ! ye children, blithe and merry,
   This one Child your model make ;
Christmas holly, leaf, and berry,
   All be prized for His dear sake ;
Come ! ye gentle hearts and tender ;
   Come ! ye spirits keen and bold ;
All in all your homage render,
   Weak and mighty, young and old.

High above a star is shining,
   And the Wise Men haste from far :
Come ! glad hearts, and spirits pining :
   For you all has risen the Star.
Let us bring our poor oblations,
   Thanks, and love, and faith, and praise :
Come ! ye people, come ! ye nations,
   All in all draw nigh to gaze.

Hark ! the heaven of heavens is ringing —
   Christ the Lord to man is born :
Are not all our hearts, too, singing —
   Welcome, welcome, Christmas morn ?
Still the Child, all power possessing,
   Smiles as through the ages past ;
And the song of Christmas-blessing
   Sweetly sinks to rest at last.

THE INFANT JESUS.

DEAR little One! how sweet Thou art,
   Thine eyes how bright they shine,
   So bright, they almost seem to speak
When Mary's look meets Thine!

When Mary bids Thee sleep, Thou sleep'st,
   Thou wakest when she calls;
Thou art content upon her lap,
   Or in the rugged stalls.

Simplest of Babes! with what a grace
   Thou dost Thy mother's will!
Thine infant fashions well betray
   The Godhead's hidden skill.

When Joseph takes Thee in his arms,
   And smooths Thy little cheek,
Thou lookest up into his face
   So helpless and so meek.

Yes! Thou art what Thou seem'st to be,
  A thing of smiles and tears;
Yet Thou art God, and heaven and earth
  Adore Thee with their fears.

Yes! dearest Babe! those tiny hands,
  That play with Mary's hair,
The weight of all the mighty world
  This very moment bear.

Art Thou, weak Babe, my very God?
  O I must love Thee then, —
Love Thee, and yearn to spread Thy love
  Among forgetful men.

MIDNIGHT CHRISTMAS COMMUNION.

OUT on the world, unheeded, came there
    One at midnight hour,
  A lowly maid His mother, and a
    manger-stall His bed ;
Out on the cold, cold winter, when the snow
    lay on the ground,
  He came a tender Infant to Bethlehem's
    humble shed.

Out on the world, unheeded — none knew
    that He was God,
  Save His parents, and the shepherds, and the
    strangers from afar ;
These were His sole adorers — the courtiers of
    the King,
  The world saw not the rising of the bright
    and morning Star.

Out on the world, forsaken, poor, He comes to
    sinners still,
  When storms are raging fiercely, and 't is
    night because of sin ;
Out on the cold, cold winter — to their thank-
    less hearts He comes,
  And they turn their faces from Him, and will
    not take Him in.

Out on the world, neglected — careless Chris-
    tians love Him not
  While in our temples dwelling, veiled in
    mystery most high ;
Unbelieving they reject Him — they will not
    own their Lord,
  Out on the cold, cold winter — for they pass
    unmindful by.

But every lowly bosom which receives him
    tenderly
  He strengthens with His presence, and His
    blessing comfort brings ;
What joy to that poor dwelling when the Lord
    of Glory comes —
  Another Bethlehem's manger to enthrone the
    King of kings.

Such be my heart, dear Jesus, this blessed
    Christmas morn;
  Cold, cold the world unheeding, but my
    Guest vouchsafe to be;
Though mean and poor the dwelling, true my
    heart's glad welcome is,
  And this my prayer unceasing — Stay Thou
    evermore with me.

Out on the world, forsaken — Oh, regard Thy
    children's love —
  Our tears be reparation for the slights upon
    Thee thrown;
May the Church's great salvation, Thy holy
    sacrifice,
  Avail for all the thankless, and for all our
    sins atone.

Alleluia! Alleluia! Till death our voices hush,
  Till we join the Church triumphant, and
    reach the Fount of grace;
There no more the hidden presence, nor Eu-
    charistic rite,
  But the Bridegroom's marriage supper, and
    to see Him face to face.

A CAROL FOR CHRISTMAS-TIDE.

NOW lift the carol, men and maids,
   Now make exultant singing,
   This day the Well of Life first sprang —
Who shall declare its springing?
It is the birthday of our Peace;
   This day for man, the weary,
The everlasting Son of God
   Was born of blessed Mary.

He was not born in such sweet days
   As we of yore remember;
It was not sunny summer-time,
   Oh, it was bleak December:
Over our heads the sun is bright,
   Beneath the snowfalls slacken,
So, unto this dark wintry world
   He came, the dead to quicken.

He did not bring a royal train,
  A host no man could number ;
Nor lay begirt by damask folds,
  Nor lulled by harp to slumber ;
Oh, He was wrapped in swathing bands
  Whose might o'erspans the heaven,
And a poor trough, whence oxen fed,
  For His first rest was given.

He lies not in the manger now —
  Far o'er the sapphire portal
At the right hand of Power He sits,
  Who was this day made mortal :
All in the highest, holiest place,
  Where there may dwell none other,
There our own Manhood sits enthroned,
  There is our Elder Brother.

The birthday of our God and King —
  Lo! we are called to greet Him ;
The everlasting Bridegroom comes,
  Oh, go ye out to meet Him.
This is the end of all below,
  The crown of Love's best story ;
Christ stands and knocks — oh, happy souls,
  Receive the King of Glory.

GOOD FRIDAY.

ESU, mighty Sufferer! say,
How shall we this dreadful day
Near Thee draw, and to Thee pray?

We, whose proneness to forget
Thy dear love, on Olivet,
Bathed Thy brow with bloody sweat; —

We, who still in thought and deed
Often hold the bitter reed
To Thee, in Thy time of need; —

Canst Thou pardon us, and pray,
As for those who on this day
Took Thy precious life away?

Yes, Thy blood is all my plea ;
It was shed, and shed for me,
Therefore to Thy cross I flee.

Jesu, deign in love to take
Pity on my soul, and make
This day bright for Thy dear sake.

7

THE CHASTISEMENT OF OUR PEACE
WAS UPON HIM.

DARKLY rose the guilty morning,
When, the King of Glory scorning
　Raged the fierce Jerusalem :
See the Christ, His Cross upbearing,
See Him stricken, spit on, wearing
　The thorn-platted diadem.

Not the crowd whose cries assailed Him,
Not the hands that rudely nailed Him,
　Slew Him on the cursèd tree ;
Ours the sin from Heaven that called Him,
Ours the sin whose burden galled Him
　In the sad Gethsemane.

For our sins, of glory emptied,
He was fasting, lone, and tempted,
　He was slain on Calvary ;
Yet He for His murderers pleaded, —
Lord, by us that prayer is needed ;
　We have pierced, yet trust in Thee.

In our wealth and tribulation,
By Thy precious Cross and passion,
  By Thy blood and agony,
By Thy glorious resurrection,
By Thy Holy Ghost's protection,
  Make us Thine eternally.

A FINE DAY IN PASSION WEEK.

THERE is a rapturous movement, a green
     growing
  Among the hills and valleys once again,
And silent rivers of delight are flowing
    Into the hearts of men.

There is a purple weaving on the heather,
  Night drops down starry gold upon the furze,
Wild rivers and wild birds sing songs together,
  Dead Nature breathes and stirs.

Is this the season when our hearts should follow
  The Man of Sorrows to the hill of scorn?
Must not our pilgrim grief be scant and hollow
  On such a sunny morn?

Will not the silver trumpet of the river
  Wind us to gladsomeness against our will —
The subtle eloquence of sunlight shiver
  What sadness haunts us still?

If I might choose, those notes should all be
    duller,
  That silver trump should fail in Passion
    Week;
The mountain-crowning sky wear one pale
    color,
    Pale as my Saviour's cheek.

And day and night there should be one slow
    raining,
  With mournful plash, upon the moor and
    moss,
And on the hill one tree its bare arms straining,
    Bare as my Saviour's Cross.

Nay! if thy heart were sorrowful exceeding,
  Its pulses big with that divinest woe,
These natural things would only set it bleeding
    To think it could be so;

To think that guilty and degraded Nature
  Could look as joyful as she looketh now,
When the warm blood has dropped from her
    Creator
    Upon her branded brow.

Was Crucified, Dead, and Buried.

THE VIGIL.

"*When my heart is over-whelmed, lead me to the Rock that is higher than I.*"— PSALM lxi. 2.

FATHER, my cup is full !
  My trembling soul I raise ;
  Oh, save me in this solemn hour,
Thy might and love to praise !

Father, my cup is full !
  But One hath drunk before,
And for our sins Thy face was hid,
  When the bitter draught ran o'er.

Father, my cup is full !
  But Thou dost bid me drink ;
I know Thy love the chalice mixed,
  And yet I faint — I shrink.

Alone He drank the cup,
  The holy, sinless One,
That not one soul on earth again
  Should drain the dregs alone.

Father, forsake me not !
  Oh, Christ ! I look to Thee ;
And by Thy midnight agony,
  Do Thou remember me.

GETHSEMANE.

JESUS, while He dwelt below,
  As divine historians say,
  To a place would often go;
Near to Kedron's brook it lay;
In this place He loved to be;
And 't was named Gethsemane.

'T was a garden, as we read,
  At the foot of Olivet,
Low, and proper to be made
  The Redeemer's lone retreat:
When from noise He would be free,
Then He sought Gethsemane.

Thither, by their Master brought,
  His disciples likewise came;
There the heavenly truths He taught
  Often set their hearts on flame;
Therefore they, as well as He,
Visited Gethsemane.

Came at length the dreadful night;
   Vengeance, with its iron rod,
Stood, and with collected might,
   Bruised the harmless Lamb of God;
See, my soul, thy Saviour see,
Prostrate in Gethsemane.

View Him in that olive-press,
   Wrung with anguish, 'whelm'd in blood!
Hear Him pray in His distress,
   With strong cries and tears, to God:
Then reflect what sin must be,
Gazing on Gethsemane.

Gloomy garden, on thy beds,
   Wash'd by Kedron's water-pool,
Grow most rank and bitter weeds,
   Think on these, my soul, my soul!
Would'st thou sin's dominion see?
Call to mind Gethsemane.

Hither, Lord, Thou didst resort
   Oft-times with Thy little train;
Here would'st keep Thy private court,
   Oh! confer that grace again:
Lord, resort with worthless me
Oft-times to Gethsemane.

True, I can't deserve to share
    In a favor so divine ;
But since sin first fix'd Thee there,
    None have greater sins than mine ;
And to this my woful plea,
Witness thou, Gethsemane !

Sins against a holy God ;
    Sins against His righteous laws ;
Sins against His love, His blood,
    Sins against His name and cause,
Sins immense as is the sea :
— Hide me, O Gethsemane !

Saviour, all the stone remove
    From my flinty, frozen heart ;
Thaw it with the beams of love,
    Pierce it with Thy mercy's dart ;
Wound the heart that wounded Thee ;
Break it in Gethsemane !

AN ANCIENT HYMN FOR MAUNDAY-THURSDAY: FROM THE GERMAN.

IN those dark hours of bitter woe,
   When depths of agony
   Bound Me to dust, I bade it flow —
My blood, in streams for thee :
I stood alone, My hands were bound ;
   Beneath the scourge I stood ;
From their long furrows to the ground
   Fast fell the Holy blood.
My child, oh, this was all for thee ;
Oh, hast thou ever thought of Me ?

They put on Me a robe of scorn,
   Bade thorns My crown to be ;
I gladly bore it, could have borne
   More still for love of thee ;
They gave Me then the cross to bear,
   And many a word was said

Against My holy name, but ne'er—
  Love from My heart ne'er fled.
My child, oh, this was all for thee;
Oh, hast thou ever thought of Me?

The Gentile's spear hath pierced My side;
  Lo! from My heart within
Water and blood, a priceless tide,
  Flow forth to cleanse from sin.
Have I left anything undone,
  So thou by it might'st be
Brought back, My lost, My loved one?
  Have I not died for thee?
My child, oh, this was all for thee;
Oh, hast thou ever thought of Me?

For thee I was content to die,
  To shame and anguish moved;
And now, upon My throne on high
  I love as then I loved;
To thee My flesh and blood are given—
  The pure soul's mystic food—
And thou shalt be with Me in heaven
  When thou hast pass'd death's flood.
My child, oh, this was all for thee;
Oh, hast thou ever thought of Me?

AT THE LORD'S FEAST.

 COME, O Lord, to Thy dear face,
Weary and laden, seeking grace.
My God ; my Refuge ; show to me
Thy miracle of mercy free.
Behold me here before Thy throne,
Thou God in flesh and suffering shown,
To find my rest in Thee alone ;
I feel the heavy weight of sin,
I long for peace, and here begin
To taste its heavenly feast within.

To Thee I pray, in hopeful trust,
All spotted o'er with earthly dust ;
For Thou hast blotted out my stain,
And made me Thine own child again.
I think of all Thy suffering's power,
Thy precious words in Thy last hour,
Thine anguish mighty to redeem,
Thy heart's most precious saving stream,

To reconcile the world to Thee ;
Emmanuel, God with us, with me.

Rejoice in Him, rejoice, my soul,
He makes thee new, and white, and whole ;
He at His table bids thee rest,
In His dear Home a welcome guest.
Ere thou canst call, His answer mild
Replies to thee, " Take courage, child ;
Thou art forgiven, in Me despised,
Into My death thou art baptized."
Arising from that healing flood
Praise with thy life His precious blood.

" Eternal life is now thy part.
By no false trust, or Satan's art,
By no delusive smile or frown,
Let man or devil take thy crown.
I make now My abode in thee ;
I am the Vine — abide in Me ;
So shalt thou yield abundant fruit,
Growing in Me, thy stock and root."

Yes, Lord ! my joy is in Thy Law,
Which kings and prophets never saw.

Thy wondrous sacrifice shall still
Give triumph to my halting will.
O make me worthy, from this day,
On Thee my trembling heart to stay;
May true repentance ever prove
The sanctifying power of love.
Prolong Thou my unworthy breath
To honor Thy life-giving death.

TOUCHED WITH A FEELING OF OUR INFIRMITIES.

WHEN, wounded sore, the stricken soul
　　Lies bleeding and unbound,
Only one Hand, a piercèd Hand,
　　Can salve the sinner's wound.

When sorrow swells the laden breast,
　　And tears of anguish flow,
One only Heart, a broken Heart,
　　Can feel the sinner's woe.

When penitence has wept in vain
　　Over some foul dark spot,
One only stream, a stream of blood,
　　Can wash away the blot.

'T is Jesus' blood that washes white,
　　His Hand that brings relief,
His Heart that 's touched with all our joys,
　　And feeleth for our grief.

Lift up Thy bleeding Hand, O Lord,
  Unseal the cleansing tide ;
We have no shelter from our sin
  But in Thy wounded side.

8

NOT OUR WORK.

WEARY, working, plodding one,
Wherefore toil you so?
Cease your " doing ; " all was done
Long, long ago !
Jesus, from His lofty throne,
Stooped to do and die ;
Everything was fully done —
" 'T is finished ! " was His cry.
Jesus paid it all !
All that e'er was due.
And nothing either great or small
Remains for me to do !

Till to Jesus' work you cling,
By a simple faith,
" Doing " is a deadly thing,
" Doing " ends in death.
Cast your deadly " doing " down,
Down at Jesus' feet ;
Stand in Him, in Him alone,
Glorious and complete !
Jesus paid it all !

THE GRIEF OF PLEASURES.

HROUGH miry paths I labored on ;
  Dark fell the mist, I could not see ;
  But when my feet were almost gone,
A Voice said — Turn, and look on Me.

Who com'st Thou, taunted like a thief
  By hard men, joyous in Thy fall ?
Who art Thou, yearning pale with grief
  To some friend in the Judgment-hall ?

O glance too kind for broken vow,
  For crime sinned often and afresh !
O thorns, that wring the purest brow
  Made ever yet from human flesh !

O printed hands, O printed feet,
  O side, dug to the quick with steel !
I marvel, but no answering heat
  Strikes through my breast, to make it feel.

Ah, Lord ! but if Thy grace impart
  True sorrow for my inward stain,
That look will pierce me to the heart,
  That crown will tear me to the brain.

Those marks upon Thy feet and hands,
  That furrow in Thy sinless side,
Will sear me as with iron brands
  While I with Thee hang crucified.

Nay, but the world — too far, too much
  She lures me with her power to please.
How can I bear Thy healing touch
  To rob me of my sweet disease ?

I bathe me in a false delight,
  Chew dust for bread : yet, Lord, I pray,
Come, for without Thee day is night,
  Come now, for with Thee night is day.

Yea, by Thy love, Thy toil to save,
  Thy prayer, Thy groans, Thy bloody sweat,
Thy death, Thy rising from the grave,
  Look down from heaven, and hear me yet.

THE HEALER.

WHEN across the heart deep waves of
    sorrow
      Break, as on a dry and barren shore ;
When hope glistens with no bright to-morrow,
    And the storm seems sweeping evermore ;

When the cup of every earthly gladness
    Bears no taste of the life-giving stream,
And high hopes, as though to mock our sadness,
    Fade and die as in some fitful dream ;

Who shall hush the weary spirit's chiding,
    Who the aching void within shall fill ?
Who shall whisper of a peace abiding,
    And each surging billow calmly still ?

Only He whose wounded heart was broken
    With the bitter cross and thorny crown,
Whose dear love glad words of joy had spoken,
    Who His life for us laid meekly down.

Blessed Healer ! all our burdens lighten ;
　Give us peace, Thine own sweet peace, we
　　pray ;
Keep us near Thee till the Morn shall brighten,
　And all mists and shadows flee away.

"MADE NIGH, BY THE BLOOD OF CHRIST."

THIRST, Thou wounded Lamb of
God,
To wash me in Thy cleansing blood,
To dwell within Thy wounds ; then pain
Is sweet, and life or death is gain.

Take my poor heart, and let it be
Forever closed to all but Thee !
Seal Thou my breast, and let me wear
That pledge of love forever there.

How blest are they who still abide
Close shelter'd in Thy bleeding side !
Who life and strength from Thee derive,
And by Thee move, and in Thee live !

What are our works but sin and death,
Till Thou Thy quick'ning Spirit breathe !

Thou giv'st the power Thy grace to move —
O wondrous grace ! O boundless love !

Ah, Lord ! enlarge our scanty thought,
To know the wonders Thou hast wrought !
Unloose our stammering tongues, to tell
Thy love, immense, unsearchable !

First-born of many brethren Thou,
To Thee, lo ! all our souls we bow,
To Thee our hearts and hands we give :
Thine may we die, Thine may we live !

LATUS SALVATORIS.

THERE is an everlasting home,
    Where contrite souls may hide ;
Where death and danger dare not
        come —
The Saviour's side.

It was a cleft of matchless love,
    Opened when He had died,
When Mercy hailed in worlds above
        That wounded side.

Hail ! Rock of Ages, pierced for me,
    The grave of all my pride ;
Hope, peace, and heaven, are all in Thee,
        Thy sheltering side.

There issued forth the double flood,
    The sin-atoning tide,
In streams of water and of blood,
        From that dear side.

There is the only Fount of Bliss,
   In joy and sorrow tried ;
No refuge for the heart like this, —
   A Saviour's side.

Thither the Church, through all her days,
   Points as a faithful guide,
And celebrates with ceaseless praise
   That spear-pierced side.

THE CROSS AND .THE HEART.

At Sorrento, Italy, is a curious poetical inscription engraved on a slab of marble in the outer wall of a church. It begins and ends alternately with the Italian words for Cross and Heart. The following is as near as possible to a literal translation.

CROSS, most adored! to thee I give my
    heart ;
  Heart I have not, except to love the
cross.
Cross, thou hast won my wayward, alien heart ;
  Heart, thou hast owned the triumph of the
    cross.
Cross ! tree of life ! to thee I nail my heart ;
  Heart cannot live that lives not on the cross.
Cross, be thy blood the cleansing of my heart ;
  Heart, be thy blood an offering to the cross.
Cross, thou shalt have the homage of my heart ;
  Heart, thou shalt be the temple of the cross.

Cross, blest is he who yields to thee his heart ;
　　Heart, rest secure who cleavest to the cross.
Cross, key of heaven, open every heart ;
　　Heart, every heart, receive the holy cross.

THE BREAD THAT COMETH DOWN
FROM HEAVEN.

THE sun is sinking in the west;
　　And while its rays decline,
　　Gleams of the full-orbed Paschal moon
On the calm waters shine.

The Galilean waters hushed
　　In eventide are still;
Yet crowds of weary wanderers wait
　　Upon its lonely hill.

Pilgrims they are, for Sion bound,
　　Whose Paschal Feast is near;
But the true Passover Himself
　　Receives and feeds them here.

They sit upon the grassy turf,
　　Marshalled in groups and rows;
Christ holds the food, which in His hand,
　　And by His blessing grows.

He gives the food ; Apostles take,
Distribute it, and then —
Two fishes and five barley loaves
Regale five thousand men.

O blessed Lord, the earth is Thine,
By Thy creative hand
The golden harvests crown the year
And deck the fertile land.

O blessed Lord, Thou Bread of Life,
That cometh down from heaven,
Supplies of everlasting Good
By Thee to man are given.

In channels formed by Thee, they flow
In rivulets of grace,
Refreshing all who wander here
In this world's desert place.

Oh, feed us, weary pilgrims, Lord,
And to Thy Sion bring,
To keep a heavenly feast with Thee,
Our Prophet, Priest, and King.

THE MIRACLES OF GRACE AND NATURE.

MYSTERIOUS is Thy presence, Lord,
　　Awful Thy power divine ;
　　The water hears Thy faintest word,
And blushes into wine.

The clouds, that round us dark and low,
　　With threatening aspect move,
If Thou dost look upon them, glow
　　With rainbow lights of love.

The grain, that from the sower's hand
　　Is scattered on the mould,
Soon in the valleys thick shall stand,
　　Returned a thousand-fold.

The dews, which evening skies distil
　　Around the creeping vine,
At Thy command arise and fill
　　The blood-red grape with wine.

Thus holy truths around us lie,
Doing their humble part,
But wanting the attentive eye,
And the believing heart.

Thus at Thy holy Feast, O Lord,
We kneel, and we believe
That that which Thy creative word
Hath made it, we receive.

Mysterious truth, which human pride
Must bow to and adore,
Which in our heart of hearts we hide,
Believe, and ask no more.

THE CHRISTIAN ALTAR.

HOU Bread of Life, upon Thy tongue
When famished thousands closely hung,
Didst make the fainting body whole :
Come, strengthen and refresh our soul.

Thou, when the bridal wine ran dry,
A draught far richer didst supply :
With real fulness of that hour,
Come, cheer our souls, Thy blood outpour.

So bid us from Thy board depart,
With all Thy presence in our heart,
And bear it far into the night
Of world and sin, Thy Lamp of Light.

5

THE OBLATION.

NCE I thought to sit so high
In the palace of the sky ;
Now, I thank God for His grace,
If I may fill the lowest place.

Once I thought to scale so soon
Heights above the changing moon ;
Now, I thank God for delay —
To-day, it yet is called to-day.

While I stumble, halt and blind,
Lo ! he waiteth to be kind ;
Bless me soon, or bless me slow,
Except He bless, I let not go.

Once for earth I laid my plan,
Once I leaned on strength of man,
When my hope was swept aside,
I stayed my broken heart on pride :

Broken reed hath pierced my hand ;
Fell my house I built on sand ;
Roofless, wounded, maimed by sin,
Fightings without and fears within :

Yet, a tree, He feeds my root ;
Yet, a branch, He prunes for fruit ;
Yet, a sheep, these eves and morns
He seeks for me among the thorns.

With Thine Image stamped of old,
Find Thy coin more choice than gold ;
Known to Thee by name, recall
To Thee Thy home-sick prodigal.

Sacrifice and offering
None there is that I can bring ;
None, save what is Thine alone :
I bring Thee, Lord, but of Thine own —

Broken body, blood outpoured,
These I bring, my God, my Lord ;
Wine of Life, and Living bread,
With these for me Thy board is spread.

THE HOLY FEAST.

LO ! the feast is spread to-day,
Jesus summons, come away
From the vanity of life,
From the sounds of mirth or strife,
To the feast by Jesus given,
Come and taste the Bread of Heaven.

Why, with proud excuse and vain,
Spurn His mercy once again ?
From amidst life's social ties,
From the farm and merchandise,
Come, for all is now prepared ;
Freely given, be freely shared.

Blessed are the lips that taste
Our Redeemer's Marriage-feast ;
Blessed, who on Him shall feed,
Bread of Life, and Drink indeed ;
Blessed, for their thirst is o'er ;
They shall never hunger more.

THE HUNGER.

LORD, to Thine altar let me go,
The child of weariness and woe,
My home to find ;
From sin, and sense, and self set free,
Absorbed alone in love to Thee,
Able to leave in liberty
This world behind.

Jesus, be Thou my Heavenly Food,
Sweet Source Divine of every good,
Centre of rest ;
One with Thy heart let me be found,
Prostrate upon that holy ground,
Where grace, and peace, and life abound,
Drawn from Thy breast.

There let me lean, and live, and lie,
As fast the fleeting moments fly,
Sands in a glass,
Which Time may shake with restless hand,
Yet only at Thine own command,
Till to a dearer, happier Land,
My soul shall pass.

THE MORNING OF RECEPTION.

IT is a day of fear :
　　Rise up betimes, go forth alone
　　With tongue fast sealed and heart
　　　　bowed down,
Because Thy Lord is near.

Leave not thy thoughts to roam
Hither and thither, where they would ;
Lest fretful cares on thee should crowd,
　　Forgetful of thy Home.

Let not thine eye go free ;
Look on the earth beneath thy feet,
The pit that for thy sins was meet,
　　Had God been just with thee.

Good art thou to the sight ;
But would thy cheek be dry as now,
As gay thy smile, as bright thy brow,
　　If all were brought to light ?

Yet, not in gloomy sadness
Be thy heart bowed and eye downcast ;
Is not the night of sorrow past ?
  Is 't not a morn of gladness ?

Think on the Holy Feast,
On His dear love and gracious Name
Who sanctifies Himself, the same
  Both Sacrifice and Priest.

Go, and be one with Him ;
Dwell thou in Him, and He in thee,
Him freely love, who sets thee free,
  Though but in shadow dim.

For, it shall not be so
In that great day, when faithful souls,
Whom flesh doth sway and sin controls,
  As they are known shall know :

To be forever one
With Him, whom with the Father high,
And Spirit, angels tremblingly
  Adore as God alone.

THIS DO IN REMEMBRANCE OF ME.

HERE, O my Lord, I see Thee face to
    face ;
    Here would I touch and handle things
       unseen ;
Here grasp with firmer hand the eternal grace,
    And all my weariness upon Thee lean.

Here would I feed upon the bread of God ;
    Here drink with Thee the royal wine of
       Heaven ;
Here would I lay aside each earthly load,
    Here taste afresh the calm of sin forgiven.

This is the hour of banquet and of song,
    This is the heavenly table spread for me ;
Here let me feast, and, feasting, still prolong
    The brief bright hour of fellowship with
       Thee.

Too soon we rise ; the symbols disappear ;
    The feast, though not the love, is passed and
       gone ;

The bread and wine remove, but Thou art
    here,
  Nearer than ever, still my Shield and Sun.

I have no help but Thine; nor do I need
  Another arm save Thine to lean upon;
It is enough, my Lord, enough, indeed:
  My strength is in Thy might, Thy might
    alone.

I have no wisdom, save in Him who is
  My wisdom and my teacher, both in one;
No wisdom can I lack while Thou art wise,
  No teaching do I crave, save Thine alone.

Mine is the sin, but Thine the righteousness;
  Mine is the guilt, but Thine the cleansing
    blood;
Here is my robe, my refuge, and my peace,—
  Thy blood, Thy righteousness, O Lord my
    God.

I know that deadly evils compass me,
  Dark perils threaten; yet I would not fear,
Nor poorly shrink, nor feebly turn to flee;
  Thou, O my Christ, art buckler, sword,
    spear.

But see, the Pillar-cloud is rising now,
  And moving onward through the desert-night ;
It beckons, and I follow, for I know
  It leads me to the heritage of light.

Feast after feast thus comes and passes by ;
  Yet, passing, points to the glad feast above,
Giving sweet foretaste of the festal joy,
  The Lamb's great Bridal Feast of bliss and
    love.

THE TRUE BREAD.

TRUE Bread of life, in pitying mercy given,
  Long-famished souls to strengthen and
    to feed ;
Christ Jesus, Son of God, true Bread of
    Heaven,
  Thy Flesh is meat, Thy Blood is drink in-
    deed.

I cannot famish, though this earth should fail,
  Though life through all its fields should pine
    and die ;
Though the sweet verdure should forsake each
    vale,
  And every stream of every land run dry.

True Tree of life ! of Thee I eat and live, —
  Who eateth of Thy fruit shall never die ;
'T is Thine the everlasting health to give,
  The youth and bloom of immortality.

Feeding on Thee, all weakness turns to power,
  This sickly soul revives, like earth in spring;
Strength floweth on and in, each buoyant hour,
  This being seems all energy, all wing.

Jesus, our dying, buried, risen Head,
  Thy Church's Life and Lord, Immanuel!
At Thy dear Cross we find the eternal bread,
  And in Thy empty tomb the living well.

AND WHEN THEY HAD SUNG AN HYMN, THEY WENT OUT UNTO THE MOUNT OF OLIVES.

CALM lay the city in its double sleep,
　　Beneath the Paschal Moon's cold,
　　　　silvery light,
That flung broad shadows o'er the rugged steep
　　Of Olivet that night.

But soon the calm was broken, and the sound
　　Of strains all sweet and plaintive filled the air ;
And deep-toned voices, echoing all around,
　　Made music everywhere.

The Holy Rite is o'er ; the Blessed Sign
　　Is given to cheer us in this earthly strife ;
The Bread is broken, and outpoured the Wine,—
　　Symbol of better Life.

The bitter cup of wrath before Him lies ;
　　And yet as up the steep they pass along,

The mighty Victim to the Sacrifice,
They cheer the way with song.

We ne'er can know such sorrow as that night
Pierced to the heart the suffering Son of God ;
And every earthly sadness is but light
To that dark path He trod !

And yet how faint and feeble rise our songs ;
How oft we linger 'mid the shadows dim ;
Nor give the glory that to Him belongs
In Eucharistic hymn !

O for an echo of that chant of praise ;
O for a voice to sing His mighty love ;
O for a refrain of the hymns they raise
In the bright Home above !

Touch Thou our wayward hearts, and let them
be
In stronger faith to Thy glad service given,
Till, o 'er the margin of Time's surging sea,
We sing the song of Heaven !

HOLY COMMUNION.

WITH all the powers my poor soul hath
Of humble love, and loyal faith,
I come, dear Lord, to worship Thee,
Whom so much love bowed low for me.

Down, busy sense ; discourses die ;
And all adore faith's mystery !
Faith is my skill, faith can believe
As fast as love new laws shall give.

Faith is my eye, faith strength affords
To keep pace with those gracious words ;
And words more sure, more sweet than they,
Love could not think, truth could not say.

O dear memorial of that Death
Which still survives, and gives us breath !
Live ever, Bread of Life, and be
My food, my joy, my all to me !

Come, glorious Lord! my hopes increase,
And mix my portion with Thy peace!
Come, and forever dwell in me
That I may only live to Thee!

Come, hidden life, and that long day
For which I languish, come away!
When this dry soul those eyes shall see,
And drink the unsealed Source of Thee;

When Glory's Sun faith's shade shall chase,
And for Thy veil, give me Thy face;
Then shall my praise eternal be
To the Eternal Trinity!

COMMUNION HYMN.

HE cometh, on yon hallowed Board
   The ready Feast doth duly show,
Where wait the chalice and the
   bread,
Like gems within their veil of snow.

He cometh, as He came of old,
   Suddenly to His Father's shrine,
Into the hearts He died to make
   Meet temples for His grace Divine.

He cometh, as the Bridegroom comes,
   Unto the Feast Himself has spread;
His flesh and blood the heavenly food
   Wherewith the wedding guests are fed.

He cometh — gentle as the dew,
   And sweet as drops of honey clear,
And good as God's own manna shower,
   To longing souls that meet Him here.

He cometh — let not one withdraw,
  Nor fear to bring repented sin ;
There 's blood to wash, there 's bread to feed,
  And Christ Himself to enter in.

He cometh — praises in the Church,
  And hymns of praise in Heaven above,
And in our hearts repentant faith,
  And love that springs to meet His love.

II.

O Jesu, bruised and wounded more
  Than bursted grape, or bread of wheat ;
The Life of Life within our souls,
  The Cup of our Salvation sweet ;

We come to show Thy dying hour,
  Thy streaming vein, Thy broken flesh ;
And still the blood is warm to save,
  And still the fragrant wounds are fresh.

O Heart that, with a double tide
  Of blood and water, maketh pure ;
O Flesh once offered on the Cross,
  The gift that makes our pardon sure :

Let never more our sinful souls
  The anguish of Thy Cross renew ;
Nor forge again the cruel nails
  That pierced Thy victim Body through.

Come, Bread of Heaven, to feed our souls,
  And with Thee, Jesu enter in ;
Come, Wine of God, and as we drink
  His precious blood, wash out our sin.

THE HOLY COMMUNION.

NO Gospel like this Feast
          Spread for Thy Church by Thee ;
     Nor prophet nor evangelist
Preach the glad news so free.

All our Redemption cost,
  ' All our Redemption won ;
All it has won for us, the lost,—
     All it cost Thee, the Son ; —

Thine was the bitter price,
     Ours is the free gift given ;
Thine was the Blood of Sacrifice,
     Ours is the wine of Heaven !

For Thee, the burning thirst,
     The shame, the mortal strife,
The broken heart, the side transpierced ;
     To us, the Bread of Life !

To Thee, our curse and doom
     Wrapt round Thee with our sin ;

The horror of that mid-day gloom,
  The deeper night within.

To us, Thy home in light,
  Thy " Come, ye blessed, come ! "
Thy bridal raiment pure and white,
  Thy Father's welcome home.

Here we would rest midway,
  As on a sacred height,
That darkest and that brightest Day
  Meeting before our sight ;

From that dark depth of woes
  Thy love for us hath trod,
Up to the heights of blest repose
  Thy love prepares with God :

Till, from self's chains released,
  One sight alone we see, —
Still at the Cross, as at the Feast,
  Behold Thee, only Thee !

THE COMPLETION OF THE SACRIFICE
OF THE CROSS.

WERE it from my heart alone
   Praise ascended to Thy throne,
   Were there not within its shrine
More than earthly bread and wine,
Then, O then, it could not bless
Save by owning thanklessness.

Wake, my glory ; wake, sweet string ;
I myself will wake and sing ;
Lo ! my heart forgets its care,
For my love hath entered there,
And its only thought is this —
He is mine, and I am His !

What the fathers longed to see,
And the prophets' company,
What the holy kings long dead
Their true Crown had reckonèd,

The most holy Bread of Heaven —
This to me is freely given.

What the people on the shore
Prayed might feed them evermore,
What the woman by the well
Asked, that she might thirstless dwell,
This is rendered to our need —
Meat indeed and Drink indeed.

Who shall measure out its price?
Who for it make sacrifice?
Gold or rubies gauge it never,
All from all for it may sever,
And though nought to yield remain,
Infinite would be their gain.

Therefore with all hosts on high —
Alleluia ! — rapt I cry ;
Praise to Him, who from the highest
Hath to lowly souls come nighest ;
Sing of Him till time is o'er,
Alleluia ! evermore.

ROCK OF AGES — IN LATIN

JESUS, pro me perforatus,
  Condar intra Tuum latus.
    Tu per lympham profluentem,
Tu per sanguinem tepentem,
In peccata mi redunda,
Tolle culpam, sordes munda.

Coram Te, nec justus forem
Quamvis totâ si laborem,
Nec si fide nunquam cesso,
Fletu stillans indefesso :
Tibi soli tantum munus ;
Salva me, Salvator unus !

Nil in manu mecum fero,
Sed me versus crucem gero ;
Vestimenta nudus oro,
Opem debilis imploro ;
Fontem Christi quæro immundus,
Nisi laves, moribundus.

Dum hos artus vita regit ;
Quando nox sepulchro tegit ;
Mortuos cum stare jubes,
Sedens Judex inter nubes ;
Jesus, pro me perforatus,
Condar intra Tuum latus.

He Descended into Hell.

EASTER-EVE.

SILENCE in the house of prayer;
    Low our Lord in earth lies sleeping;
Silence, silence, everywhere,
While the saints their watch are keeping.

He at earliest morn shall rise;
    Now in mystic peace He slumbers;
Flow, ye plaintive melodies;
    Ring, ye still recurring numbers.

Though for us His soul doth seek
    That mysterious world of spirits,
He shall rise to cheer the weak;
    Hope and joy His Church inherits.

So Lent's latest vigil now
  Keep we with a tempered sadness :
Easter-morn ! speed quickly thou,
  And transform this grief to gladness.

VIGIL OF EASTER-EVE.

RESTING from His work to-day,
In the tomb the Saviour lay,
His sacred form from head to feet
Swathèd in the winding-sheet.
Lying in the rock alone,
Hid behind the sealèd stone.

All that seventh day long I ween
Mournful watch'd the Magdalene,
Rising early, resting late,
By the sepulchre to wait,
In the holy garden glade,
Where her buried Lord was laid.

So, as clos'd the Sabbath night,
In Goshen watch'd the Israelite,
Staff in hand, in pilgrim guise,
By the slaughter'd sacrifice,
Waiting till the midnight cry
Signal gave that God was nigh.

So with Thee, till life shall end,
I would solemn vigil spend ;
Let me hew Thee, Lord, a shrine
In this rocky heart of mine,
Where in pure embalmèd cell
None but Thou mayst ever dwell.

Still with Thee their Sabbath keep
They who 'neath the altar sleep ;
Scarce a day perchance doth seem
The time of their unbodied dream,
'Twixt their rest from labor past
And their waking at the last.

Then, the new creation done,
Shall be the endless rest begun.
Jesu ! keep me safe from sin,
That I with Thee may enter in,
And danger past, and toil at end,
To Thy resting-place ascend.

CHRIST RISEN.

ALLELUIA ! Alleluia !
  Hearts to heaven and voices raise ;
  Sing to God a hymn of gladness,
Sing to God a hymn of praise.
He who on the cross a victim
  For the world's salvation bled,
Jesus Christ, the King of Glory,
  Now is risen from the dead.

Now the iron bars are broken,
  Christ from death to life is born,
Glorious life, and life immortal,
  On this holy Easter morn :
Christ has triumphed, and we conquer
  By His mighty enterprise,
We with Christ to life eternal
  By His resurrection rise.

Christ is risen, Christ, the first-fruits
   Of the holy harvest-field,
Which will all its full abundance
   At His second coming yield ;
Then the golden ears of harvest
   Will their heads before Him wave,
Ripened by His glorious sunshine,
   From the furrows of the grave.

Christ is risen, we are risen :
   Shed upon us heavenly grace,
Rain, and dew, and gleams of glory,
   From the brightness of Thy face,
That we, Lord, with hearts in heaven,
   Here on earth may fruitful be,
And by angel-hands be gathered,
   And be ever safe with Thee.

Alleluia ! Alleluia !
   Glory be to God on high,
To the Father, and the Saviour,
   Who has gained the victory ;
Glory to the Holy Spirit,
   Fount of love and sanctity.
Alleluia ! Alleluia !
   To the Triune Majesty !

EASTER DAY.

A PATHWAY opens from the tomb,
   The grave's a grave no more !
   Stoop down : look into that sweet room :
Pass through the unsealed door :
Linger a moment by the bed,
Where lay but yesterday the Church's Head.

What is there there to make thee fear ?
   A folded chamber-vest,
   Akin to that which thou shalt wear,
   When for thy slumber drest :
Two gentle angels sitting by —
How sweet a room, methinks, wherein to lie !

No gloomy vault, no charnel cell,
   No emblems of decay,
   No solemn sound of passing bell,
   To say, " He's gone away ; " —
But angel-whispers soft and clear,
And He, the risen Jesus, standing near.

" Why weepest thou ? Whom seekest thou ?"
   'Tis not the gardener's voice,

But His to whom all knees shall bow,
  In whom all hearts rejoice ;
The voice of Him who yesterday
Within that rock was Death's resistless prey.

" Why weepest thou ?   Whom seekest thou ?
  The living with the dead ? "
Take young spring flowers and deck thy brow,
  For life with joy is wed :
The grave is now the grave no more ;
Why fear to pass that bridal-chamber door ?

Take flowers and strew them all around
  The room where Jesus lay :
But softly tread ; 't is hallowed ground,
  And this is Easter day.
" The Lord is risen," as He said,
And thou shalt rise with Him, thy risen Head.

11

HYMN FOR EASTER.

THE tomb is empty; wouldst thou have
      it full ?
    Still   sadly   clasping   the   unbreathing
      clay ; —
O weak in faith, O slow of heart and dull,
    To doat on darkness, and shut out the day !

The tomb is empty; He who, three short days,
    After a sorrowing life's long weariness,
Found refuge in this rocky resting-place,
    Has now ascended to the throne of bliss.

Here lay the Holy One, the Christ of God,
    He who for death gave death, and life for life ,
Our Heavenly Kinsman, our true flesh and blood ;
    Victor for us on hell's dark field of strife.

This was the Bethel, where, on stony bed,
    While angels went and came from morn till
      even,
Our truer Jacob laid His wearied head ;
    This was to Him the very gate of Heaven.

The Conqueror, not the conquered, He to
  whom
The keys of death and of the grave belong,
Crossed the cold threshold of the stranger's tomb,
  To spoil the spoiler and to bind the strong.

Here Death had reigned; into no tomb like
  this
Had man's fell foe aforetime found his way;
So grand a trophy ne'er before was his,
  So vast a treasure, so Divine a prey.

But now his triumph ends; the rock-barred
  door
Is opened wide, and the great Prisoner gone;
Look round and see, upon the vacant floor
  The napkin and the grave-clothes lie alone.

Yes, Death's last hope, his strongest fort and
  prison
Is shattered, never to be built again;
And He, the mighty Captive, He is risen,
  Leaving behind the gate, the bar, the chain.

Yes, He is risen who is the First and Last;
  Who was and is; Who liveth and was dead;

Beyond the reach of death He now has passed,
　Of the one glorious Church the glorious
　　Head.

The tomb is empty ; so, ere long, shall be
　The tombs of all who in this Christ repose ;
They died with Him who died upon the tree,
　They live and rise with Him who lived and
　　rose.

All that was death in them is now dissolved,
　For death can only what is death's destroy ;
And when this earth's short ages have revolved,
　The disimprisoned life comes forth with joy.

Their life-long battle with disease and pain,
　And mortal weariness, is over now ;
Youth, health, and comeliness return again,
　The tear has left the cheek, the sweat the
　　brow.

They are not tasting death, but taking rest,
　On the same holy couch where Jesus lay,
Soon to awake, all glorified and blest,
　When day has broke, and shadows fled away.

EASTER CELEBRATION.

THOU, that on the first of Easters
    Cam'st resplendent from the tomb,
Leaving all Thy linen cerements
    Folded in the cavern's gloom,
Come with Thine — All hail — to greet us,
    Come, our Paschal joy to be ;
Let our altar, clad in brightness,
    Yield a throne of white for Thee.

This shall crown the Queen of Sundays ;
    Grant but this — our cup runs o'er ;
Hymns that welcomed in Thine Easter
    Made us long for this the more :
All the Paschal Alleluias
    Craved to see the Lamb appear ;
Come the hour when faith shall tell us —
    He is risen ; He is here.

Agnus Dei, we are guilty ;
   Panis Vitæ, we are faint ;
But Thou didst not rise at Easter
   To be deaf to our complaint ;
Come, oh come, to cleanse and feed us,
   Breathing peace and kindling love,
Till Thy Paschal blessings bear us
   To the Feast of feasts above.

ASCENSION.

LIFT up your heads, ye mighty gates :
  Behold, the King of Glory waits,
  The King of kings is drawing near,
The Saviour of the world is here ;
Life and salvation doth He bring,
Rejoice aloud, and gladly sing.

Fling wide the portals of your heart ;
Make it a temple set apart
From earthly use, for heaven's employ,
Adorned with prayer, and love, and joy ;
So shall your Sovereign enter in,
And new and nobler life begin.

Redeemer, come ! we open wide
Our hearts to Thee ; here, Lord, abide !

Let us Thy inner presence feel,
Thy grace and love in us reveal:
Thy Holy Spirit guide us on,
Until the glorious crown be won!

THE CEASELESS INTERCESSION.

FATHER of Love, who didst not spare
   For us Thine only Son,
   Oh, look on Him, and hear the prayer
Of Thy poor suppliant one —

Behold His piercèd hands and feet,
   Pleading for us e'en now ;
Behold that wounded heart so sweet ;
   Behold, upon His brow,

The traces of the thorny crown ;
   Behold the stripes He bore ;
By these, He claims us for His own —
   His own, for evermore.

Oh, look on Him, and let the cry
   Of this our Brother's blood,

Who, guiltless, for our guilt did die,
  Ascend to Thee our God.

Clothed in His raiment we appear,
  Kneeling before His throne,
Besprinkled with that blood so dear
  The garment Thou wilt own.

And for its sake, the sinner vile
  Thus made Thy wedding guest,
E'en such an one as her, erewhile
  By seven fiends possessed.

No depths of sin can drown that love,
  No water quench its fire :
Desponding soul, arise, and prove
  Its might, its strong desire :

Come, yea in lowliest confidence,
  Approach in Jesu's name ;
Greater His love than all offence —
  Father, that love we claim.

Bending before Thine altar low,
  We offer it to Thee :
The purest offering earth can know,
  Or heaven look down to see.

HOMEWARD GUIDE.

JESU ! guide our way
   To eternal day !
    So shall we, no more delaying,
Follow Thee, Thy voice obeying ;
   Lead us by Thy hand
   To our Father's land !

   When we danger meet,
   Steadfast make our feet!
Lord, preserve us uncomplaining
'Mid the darkness round us reigning !
   Through adversity
   Lies our way to Thee.

   Order all our way
   Through this mortal day ;
In our toil with aid be near us ;
In our need with succor cheer us ;
   When life's course is o'er,
   Open Thou the door !

THE LORD'S KNOCKING.

THE night is far spent, and the day is at
    hand,
  There are signs in the heaven, and
    signs on the land,
In the wavering earth, and the drouth of the
    sea —
But He stands and He knocks, sinner, nearer to
    thee.

His night-winds but whisper until the day break
To the Bride, for in slumber her heart is awake :
He must knock at the sleep where the revellers
    toss
With the dint of the nails and the shock of the
    cross.

Look out at the casement ; see how He appears ;
Still weeping for thee all Gethsemane's tears ;
Ere they plait Him earth's thorns, in its solitude
  crowned,
With the drops of the night and the dews of the
  ground.

Will you wait ? Will you slumber until He is
  gone,
Till the beam of the timber cry out to the stone ;
Till He shout at thy sepulchre, tear it apart,
And knock at the dust, who would speak to thy
  heart ?

HOW LONG?

*" How long, Lord, wilt Thou hide Thyself? forever?
Return, O Lord, how long ? " — Ps. lxxxix. 46 ; xc. 13.*

HOW long, O Lord, in weariness and
   sorrow,
  Must Thy poor people tread the pil-
    grim road,
Mourning to-day and fearing for to-morrow, —
  Finding no place of rest, no sure abode ? —

Sighing o'er faded flowers and cisterns broken ;
  Gazing on setting suns, that rise no more ;
Listening to sad farewells, and last words spoken
  By loved ones leaving us on Jordan's shore !

How long, through snares of error and temp-
    tation,
  Shall noblest spirits stumble on their way ?
How long, through darkening storms of trib-
    ulation,
  Must we press forward to eternal day ?

How long shall passing faults and trifles sever
  Hearts that have known affection's holy tie ?

When shall the slanderer's tale be hushed forever,
And brethren see in all things eye to eye ?

How long shall last the night of toil and sadness,
The midnight hour of gloomy doubts and
fears ?
When shall it dawn, that promised morn of
gladness,
When Thine own hand shall wipe away our
tears ?

How long, O Lord ? Our hearts are sad and
weary,
Our voices join the whole creation's groan ;
With eager gaze we watch for Thine appearing,
When wilt Thou come again, and claim
Thine own ?

Return ! return ! come in Thy power and glory,
With all Thy risen saints and angel throng ;
Bring to a close Time's strange, mysterious
story, —
How long dost Thou delay, — O Lord, how
long ?

BEHOLD, THE BRIDEGROOM COMETH.

REJOICE, rejoice, believers !
    And let your lights appear ;
The evening is advancing,
    The darker night is near.
The Bridegroom is arising ;
    And soon will He draw nigh :
Up ! pray, and watch, and wrestle,
    At midnight comes the cry.

See that your lamps are burning,
    Replenish them with oil ;
Look now for your salvation,
    The end of sin and toil.
The watchers on the mountain
    Proclaim the Bridegroom near,
Go, meet Him as He cometh,
    With hallelujahs clear.

Oh ! wise and holy virgins,
    Now raise your voices higher,
Till, in your jubilations,
    Ye meet the angel-choir.

The Marriage Feast is waiting,
  The gates wide open stand ;
Up, up, ye heirs of glory,
  The Bridegroom is at hand.

Our hope and expectation,
  O Jesu, now appear,
Arise, Thou Sun so looked for,
  O'er this benighted sphere !
With hearts and hands uplifted,
  We plead, O Lord, to see
The day of our redemption,
  And ever be with Thee !

12

HYMN FOR ADVENT.

WHEN Jesus came to earth of old,
　　He came in weakness and in woe ;
　　He wore no form of angel mould,
But took our nature poor and low.

But when He cometh back once more,
　　There shall be set the Great White Throne,
And earth and heaven shall flee before
　　The face of Him that sits thereon.

O Son of God, in glory crowned,
　　The Judge ordained of quick and dead ;
O Son of man, so pitying found
　　For all the tears Thy people shed ; —

Be with us in this darkened place,
　　This weary, restless, dangerous night ;
And teach, O teach us by Thy grace
　　To struggle onward into light.

And since in God's recording book
　　Our sins are written every one, —

The crime, the wrath, the wandering look,
　　The good we knew, and left·undone ; —

Lord, ere the last dread trumpet sound,
　　And ere before Thy face we stand,
Look Thou on each accusing word,
　　And blot it with Thy bleeding hand.

And by the love that brought Thee here,
　　And by the Cross, and by the grave,
Give perfect love for conscious fear,
　　And in the Day of Judgment save.

And lead us on, while here we stray,
　　And make us love our heavenly home ;
Till from our hearts we learn to say,
　　" Even so, Lord Jesus, quickly come."

THE BLESSED HOPE.

COME, Lord Jesus, quickly come!
Lo, Thy Church with longing eye
Lifts her blended voices high,
Not a lip is dumb.

They who sow with many a tear
In the dry and stubborn soil,
Mourning ask from out their toil, —
"Master, art Thou near?"

Watchers of the weary night,
While they pace their lonely round,
Listen for the trumpet's sound, —
Seek the dawning light.

When shall lighten forth Thy sign
Through the heavens?   O Lord, how long?
When, amid the radiant throng,
Shall Thy coming shine?

EVEN SO COME, LORD JESUS.

COME, Lord, and tarry not ;
　　Bring the long-looked-for day ;
　　Oh, why these years of waiting
　　　　here,
These ages of delay ?

Come, for Thy saints still wait ;
　　Daily ascends their sigh ;
The Spirit and the Bride say, Come :
　　Dost Thou not hear the cry ?

Come, for creation groans,
　　Impatient of Thy stay,
Worn out with these long years of ill,
　　These ages of delay.

Come, for Thy Israel pines,
　　An exile from Thy fold ;
O call to mind Thy faithful word,
　　And bless them as of old.

Come, for love waxes cold,
　Its steps are faint and slow;
Faith now is lost in unbelief,
　Hope's lamp burns dim and low.

Come, for the corn is ripe,
　Put in Thy sickle now,
Reap the great harvest of the earth;
　Sower and reaper Thou!

Come, in Thy glorious might,
　Come with the iron rod,
Scattering Thy foes before Thy face,
　Most mighty Son of God.

Come, and make all things new,
　Build up this ruined earth,
Restore our faded Paradise,
　Creation's second birth.

Come, and begin Thy reign
　Of everlasting peace;
Come, take the kingdom to Thyself,
　Great King of Righteousness.

SURELY I COME QUICKLY.

O'ER the distant mountains breaking,
    Comes the reddening dawn of day,
    Rise, my soul, from sleep awaking,
Rise and sing, and watch and pray :
      'T is thy Saviour
On His bright returning way.

O Thou long-expected, weary
    Waits mine anxious soul for Thee,
Life is dark, and earth is dreary
    Where Thy light I do not see ;
      O my Saviour,
When wilt Thou return to me ?

Nearer is my soul's salvation,
    Spent the night, the day at hand,
Keep me in my lowly station,
    Watching for Thee till I stand,
      O my Saviour,
In Thy bright and promised land.

LIGHTED LAMPS.

SOON will the heavenly Bridegroom
  come ;
    Ye wedding-guests, draw near,
And slumber not in sin when He,
  The Son of God, is here.
With lighted lamps and oil in store
  Let every guest advance,
Nor shrink ashamed in trembling awe
  From His bright countenance.

Come, let us haste to meet our Lord,
  And hail Him with delight,
Who saved us by His precious blood,
  And sorrows infinite :
Beside Him all the patriarchs old,
  And holy prophets stand,
The glorious apostolic choir,
  The noble martyr-band.

As brethren dear they welcome us,
And lead us to the throne,
Where angels bow their veilèd heads
Before the Three in One;
Where we, with all the saints of Christ,
A white-robed multitude,
Shall praise the ascended Lord, who deigns
To wear our flesh and blood.

THE SECOND ADVENT.

BY Christ redeemed, in Christ restored,
We keep the memory adored,
And show the death of our dear Lord,
Until He come.

His fearful drops of agony,
His life-blood shed for us we see —
The wine shall tell the mystery,
Until He come.

Until the trump of God be heard,
Until the ancient graves be stirred,
And with the great commanding word,
The Lord shall come.

O blessed hope, with this elate
Let not our hearts be desolate,
But strong in faith, in patience wait,
Until He come.

I believe in the Holy Ghost.

A LITANY TO THE HOLY GHOST.

WHEN the house doth sigh and weep,
And the world is drown'd in sleep,
Yet mine eyes the watch do keep,
Sweet Spirit, comfort me !

When the passing bell doth toll,
And the furies in a shoal
Come to fright a parting soul,
Sweet Spirit, comfort me !

When the flames and hellish cries
Fright mine ears, and fright mine eyes,
And all terrors me surprise,
Sweet Spirit, comfort me !

When the Judgment is reveal'd,
And that open'd which was seal'd,
When to Thee I have appeal'd,
Sweet Spirit, comfort me !

THE SPIRIT ALSO HELPETH OUR IN-
FIRMITIES.

WHEN across the inward thought
  Comes the emptiness of life,
And it seems that earth has nought
But a vain and weary strife :

All to do, and nothing done,
  Useless days fast fleeting by,
Wanderings many, progress none,
  Faltering steps by fountains dry :

Shall we, in that hapless mood,
  Fainting fall beside the way ?
Help us Giver of all good !
  Teach Thy wretched ones to pray.

Thou that with the Father art
  One in power, in glory One,
Yet within the trusting heart
  Bearest witness with the Son :

Oh, forgive our faithless mind,
  Raise us from our low estate,

Breathe in us the will to find
  Higher life in small and great!

Give us watchful eyes and clear,
  Purgèd from the scales of sense,
Seeing still the Master near,
  And the City far from hence.

Higher lead our love and faith,
  Lower our humility;
Let the words that Jesus saith
  Be illumined all by Thee!

And in them let us discern,
  Calming all our sinful strife,
While our hearts within us burn,
  Him, the Word, the Truth, the Life!

LEAD ME AND GUIDE ME.

LEAD, kindly Light, amid the encircling
     gloom,
       Lead Thou me on !
The night is dark, and I am far from home ;
       Lead Thou me on !
Keep Thou my feet ; I do not ask to see
The distant way ; one step's enough for me.

I was not ever thus, nor prayed that Thou
       Wouldst lead me on ;
I loved to see and choose my path, but now
       Lead Thou me on !
I loved the garish day, and, spite of fears,
Pride ruled my will : remember not past years.

So long Thy power hath kept me, sure it still
       Will lead me on !
O'er moor and fen, o'er crag and torrent, till
       The night is gone,
And with the morn those angel faces smile
Which I have loved long since and lost awhile !

The Holy Catholic Church.

DAILY SERVICE OF THE CHURCH.

"And it came to pass, when Moses held up his hand, that Israel prevailed." —EXOD. xvii. 11.

ON red Rephidim's battle-plain
　　The banners sank and rose again ;
　　The tumult of the wild affray
Rolled round to Horeb's mountain gray,
Rolled down to thirsty Meribah,
　　As Israel's host swept past,
And Amalek's fierce battle-cry
　　Came surging up the blast.

Above the strife the leader hung
With hands upraised, and suppliant tongue,
And still his wearied arm was stayed,
And still the unceasing prayer was prayed,
Till evening held the setting sun
　　Wrapt in her mantle pale,
And Amalek, and all his host,
　　Rushed, routed, down the vale.

Then ask us not why, day by day,
The same sweet morning prayers we say ;
Why, night by night, our even-song
Peals in the same soft strain along ;
Why children seek the mother's knee
    At eve to lisp their prayer,
While lingers rosy-fingered sleep
    O'er their fringed eyelids fair.

Nor say, " Ye vex God's patient ear,
And vain the strains that linger here, —
A soulless form, a weary round,
A cry that hath no echoing sound ; —
Ye hear no voice, ye see no sign,
    Adown heaven's crystal stair ;
No white-robed angels gliding bring
    An answer to your prayer."

Nay, but God loves the constant cry ;
He wills the words should never die
That speak our needs.   Prayer pushes prayer
Up into heaven's sublimer air ;
There round the throne eternally
    They pass and still repass ;
Our whispers are the airs that breathe
    Above the sea of glass.

Within His temple-shrine of old
He bade the priests their watches hold ;
Still through the carven cedar flowers
The deep chant swelled at solemn hours ,
Still, day by day, the incense burning
    Crushed out its odors sweet ;
Still, morn and eve, the lamps were lighted
    Before the mercy-seat.

And Nature, with her quiet force
Of powers that keep their ordered course,
And circle on, we know not why,
Doth teach a hidden rule more high :
The dews may drop to feed the earth,
    But why should planets glow ?
Why should the golden daisy-cups
    Look yearly from below ?

Yet, night by night, so calmly pale,
The stars through heaven's blue ocean sail ;
Yet, year by year, like scattered beads,
The wild flowers come to deck our meads.
All have their places and their parts
    In heaven's sublime decrees,
And words, that seem to wander wide,
    Shall find their end like these.

ON HEARING WEEK-DAY SERVICE AT WESTMINSTER ABBEY, Sept. 1858.

FROM England's gilded halls of state
I crossed the Western Minster's gate,
And, 'mid the tombs of England's
dead,
I heard the Holy Scriptures read.

The walls around, and pillared piers,
Had stood wellnigh eight hundred years;
The words the priest gave forth had stood
Since Christ, and since before the Flood.

A thousand hearts around partook
The comfort of the Holy Book;
Ten thousand suppliant hands were spread
In lifted stone above my head.

In dust decayed the hands are gone
That fed and set the builders on;
In heedless dust the fingers lie
That hewed and heaved the stones on high;

And back to earth and air resolved
The brain that planned and poised the vault:
But undecayed, erect, and fair,
To Heaven ascends the builded Prayer,

With majesty of strength and size,
With glory of harmonious dyes,
With holy airs of heavenward thought
From floor to roof divinely fraught.

Fall down, ye bars: enlarge, my soul!
To heart's content take in the whole;
And, spurning pride's injurious thrall,
With loyal love embrace them all!

For in the presence vast and good
That bends o'er all our livelihood,
With humankind in heavenly cure,
We all are like: we all are poor.

And sure, God's poor shall never want
For service meet or seemly chant;
And for the Gospel's joyful sound
A fitting place shall still be found;

Whether the organ's solemn tones
Thrill through the dust of warriors' bones,

Or voices of the village choir
From swallow-haunted eaves aspire ;

Or, sped with healing on its wings,
The Word solicit ears of kings,
Or stir the souls, in moorland glen,
Of kingless covenanted men.

Enough for Thee, indulgent Lord,
The willing ear to hear Thy Word ;
And, time and place to match, the tale
For willing ears shall never fail.

JACOB'S LADDER.

H many a time we look on starlit nights
     Up to the sky, as Jacob did of old
    Look longing up to the eternal lights
  To spell their lines in gold.

But never more, as to the Hebrew boy,
  Each on his way the angels walk abroad ;
And never more we hear with awful joy,
  The audible voice of God.

Yet, to pure eyes the ladder still is set,
  And angel visitants still come and go,
Many bright messengers are moving yet
  From the dark world below.

Thoughts, that are red-crossed faith's outspread-
    ing wings, —
  Prayers of the Church, are keeping time and
    tryst, —
Heart-wishes, making bee-like murmurings,
  Their flower the Eucharist.

Spirits elect, through suffering rendered meet
   For those high mansions; from the nursery
      door,
Bright babes that climb up with their clay-cold
      feet,
   Unto the golden door.

These are the messengers, forever wending
   From earth to heaven, that faith alone may
      scan;
These are the angels of our God, ascending
   Upon the Son of Man.

THE LORD'S DAY.

FRESH glides the brook and blows the
    gale,
    Yet yonder halts the quiet mill!
The whining wheel, the rushing sail,
    How motionless and still!

Six days of toil, poor child of Cain,
    Thy strength the slave of Want may be;
The seventh thy limbs escape the chain, —
    A God hath made thee free!

Ah, tender was the Law that gave
    This holy respite to the breast,
To breathe the gale, to watch the wave,
    And know — the wheel may rest!

But when the waves the gentlest glide
    What image charms, to lift thine eyes?
The spire reflected on the tide
    Invites thee to the skies.

To teach the soul its nobler worth
　　This rest from mortal toils is given;
Go, snatch the brief reprieve from earth
　　And pass a guest to heaven.

They tell thee in their dreaming school,
　　Of Power from old dominion hurled,
When rich and poor, with juster rule,
　　Shall share the altered world.

Alas! since Time itself began,
　　That fable hath but fooled the hour;
Each age that ripens Power in Man,
　　But subjects Man to Power.

Yet every day in seven, at least,
　　One bright republic shall be known;—
Man's world awhile hath surely ceast,
　　When God proclaims His own!

Six days may Rank divide the poor,
　　O Dives, from thy banquet-hall;
The seventh the Father opes the door,
　　And holds His feast for all!

The Communion of Saints.

HYMN FOR ALL SAINTS' DAY.

FOR all who in Thy steadfast faith,
  And godly fear, and earnest love,
    Have from this life departed,
We bless Thy holy Name!
" Blessed are they," the Spirit saith :
They rest from all their toils, above, —
    The tried and faithful-hearted,
      Whether through martyr flame,
By Christ supported in the strife,
They upward soared to endless life,

Or with all bodily gladness dimmed
They lingered on in long disease,
    Yet, in their chamber lying,
      Have found the gate of Heaven
Most nigh, and there Thy praise have hymned
In strains that might an Angel please,

And in such peaceful dying,
    Like to the sun at even,
In solemn radiance closed their day,
To rise again with brighter ray.

For many ways hast Thou, O Lord!
Of bringing those Thou lovest home ;
    Some Thou hast swiftly stricken
        With unexpected dart : —
And some beneath the unsparing sword,
And some have gasped in ocean's foam
    The spirit that shall quicken
        Again the lifeless heart,
When, at the Archangel's trumpet blown,
They all shall stand before Thy throne.

Then shall the great and countless throng,
In solemn joy, with one accord,
    Honor and glory giving
        To Him Who sitteth there,
Raise high the new triumphant song,
" O holy, holy, holy, Lord
    Jesus forever living,
        Through Whom alone we dare
Approach the throne, Thou art the same
Who died.   We bless Thy holy Name."

THE BURIAL OF MOSES.

*" And He buried him in a valley in the land of Moab,
over against Beth-Peor: but no man knoweth of his
sepulchre unto this day."* — DEUT. xxxiv. 6.

BY Nebo's lonely mountain,
   On this side Jordan's wave,
In a vale in the land of Moab
   There lies a lonely grave.
And no man knows that sepulchre,
   And no man saw it e'er,
For the angels of God upturned the sod,
   And laid the dead man there.

That was the grandest funeral
   That ever passed on earth ;
But no man heard the trampling,
   Or saw the train go forth —
Noiselessly as the daylight
   Comes back when night is done,
And the crimson streak on ocean's cheek
   Grows into the great sun ;

 Elim, or Hymns

Noiselessly as the spring-time
  Her crown of verdure weaves,
And all the trees on all the hills
  Open their thousand leaves ;
So without sound of music,
  Or voice of them that wept,
Silently down from the mountain's crown,
  The great procession swept.

Perchance the bald old eagle,
  On gray Beth-Peor's height,
Out of his lonely eyrie
  Looked on the wondrous sight ;
Perchance the lion stalking
  Still shuns that hallow'd spot,
For beast and bird have seen and heard
  That which man knoweth not.

But when the warrior dieth,
  His comrades in the war,
With arms reversed and muffled drum,
  Follow his funeral car ;
They show the banners taken,
  They tell his battles won,
And after him lead his masterless steed,
  While peals the minute gun.

Amid the noblest of the land,
  We lay the sage to rest,
And give the bard an honored place,
  With costly marble drest,
In the great minster transept,
  Where lights like glories fall,
And the organ rings, and the sweet choir sings,
  Along the emblazoned wall.

This was the truest warrior
  That ever buckled sword ;
This, the most gifted poet
  That ever breathed a word ;
And never earth's philosopher
  Traced with his golden pen
On the deathless page truths half so sage .
  As he wrote down for men.

And had he not high honor, —
  The hill-side for a pall,
To lie in state, while angels wait
  With stars for tapers tall,
And the dark rock-pines, like tossing plumes,
  Over his bier to wave,
And God's own hand in that lonely land
  To lay him in the grave ?

In that strange grave without a name,
 Whence his uncoffined clay
Shall break again, O wondrous thought!
 Before the Judgment Day,
And stand with glory wrapped around
 On the hills he never trod,
And speak of the strife, that won our life,
 With the Incarnate Son of God.

O lonely grave in Moab's land!
 O dark Beth-Peor's hill!
Speak to these curious hearts of ours,
 And teach them to be still.
God hath His mysteries of grace,
 Ways that we cannot tell;
He hides them deep, like the hidden sleep
 Of him He loved so well.

VISION FROM THE APOCALYPSE.

I SAW again. Behold ! Heaven's open
    door ; *
Behold ! a throne, — the Seraphim
    stood o'er it, —
The white-robed elders fell upon the floor,
    And flung their crowns before it.

I saw a wondrous book — an angel strong †
    To Heaven and earth proclaimed his loud
        appeals —
But a hush passed across the seraph's song,
    For none might loose the seals.

Then, fast as rain to death-cry of the year,
    Tears of St. John to that sad cry were
        given ; ‡
It was a wondrous thing to see a tear
    Fall on the floor of Heaven.

* Rev. iv.   † Rev. v. 2.
‡ Rev. v. 4.

And a sweet voice said, " Weep not ; where-
     fore fails,
Eagle of God, thy heart, the high and leal ?
The Lion out of Judah's tribe prevails
     To loose the sevenfold seal."

'T was Israel's voice, and straightway up above
     Stood in the midst a wondrous Lamb, snow-
     white,*
Heart-wounded with the deep, sweet wounds of
     love,
     Eternal, infinite.

Then rose the song no ear had heard before ;
     Then, from the white-robed throng, high an-
     them woke ;
And fast as spring tide on the sealess shore,
     The Hallelujahs broke.

Who dreams of God when passionate youth is
     nigh,
     When first life's weary waste his feet have
     trod —
Who seeth angels' footfalls in the sky,
     Working the works of God ;

          * Rev. v. 6.

His sun shall fade as gently as it rose,
   Through the dark woof of death's approach-
       ing night;
His faith shall shoot, at life's prophetic close,*
      Some threads of golden light.

For him the silver ladder shall be set —
   His Saviour shall receive his latest breath —
He walketh to a fadeless coronet,
      Up through the gate of death!

* Heb. xi. 13.

14

WHITE ROBES AND PALMS.

WHAT countless crowd on Sion stands ?
　　Gather'd from every land and tongue,
　The palm-branch waving in their hands,
　The white robes round them flung.

These out of tribulation came ;
　On earth the thorny crown they wore ;
Believing, they confess'd His name
　Whose cross they meekly bore.

In the Lamb's life-blood wash'd they white
　Their robes, ingrain'd with sin and woe,
Now round the glory-seat in light,
　Purer they shine than snow.

Lord, when thy faithful ones indeed
　Low by remember'd sin are bow'd,
From realms where ransom'd sinners lead
　Thy choir, roll back the cloud.

Show them, in bliss before Thy throne,
   Meek tremblers once at sin's just doom,
Who, in Thy sacrifice alone,
   Found hope from wrath to come.

Sinners no more, in Thee complete,
   Their Saviour's love to man they sing;
While angels, listening, learn to greet
   With newer praise their King.

BEFORE THE THRONE.

ARK the sound of holy voices,
    Chanting at the crystal sea,
Alleluia ! Alleluia !
Alleluia ! Lord, to Thee.
Multitude which none can number,
    Like the stars, in glory stands,
Clothed in white apparel, holding
    Palms of victory in their hands.

Patriarch, and holy prophet,
    Who prepared the way of Christ,
King, apostle, saint, and martyr,
    Confessor, evangelist,
Saintly maiden, godly matron,
    Widows who have watched to prayer,
Joined in holy concert, singing
    To the Lord of all, are there.

They have come from tribulation,
   And have wash'd their robes in blood,
Washed them in the blood of Jesus ;
   Tried they were, and firm they stood ;
Mocked, imprisoned, stoned, tormented,
   Sawn asunder, slain with sword,
They have conquered Death and Satan,
   By the might of Christ the Lord.

Marching with Thy cross their banner,
   They have triumphed, following
Thee, the Captain of Salvation,
   Thee, their Saviour and their King :
Gladly, Lord, with Thee they suffered ;
   Gladly, Lord, with Thee they died ;
And by death to life immortal
   They were born, and glorified.

Now they reign in heavenly glory,
   Now they walk in golden light,
Now they drink, as from a river,
   Holy bliss and infinite ;
Love and peace they taste forever ;
   And all truth and knowledge see
In the beatific vision
   Of the blessed Trinity.

God of God, the One-begotten,
  Light of Light, Emmanuel,
In whose body joined together,
  All the saints forever dwell ;
Pour upon us of Thy fulness,
  That we may for evermore
God the Father, God the Son, and
  God the Holy Ghost adore.

"THAT WHERE I AM YE MAY BE ALSO."

LOVE craves the presence and the sight
    Of all its well-beloved ;
    And therefore weep we in the homes
Whence they are far removed ;
Love craves the presence and the sight
    Of each beloved one ;
And therefore Jesus spake the word
    Which call'd them to the throne.

Thus heaven is gathering, one by one,
    In its capacious breast,
All that is pure and permanent,
    And beautiful and blest ;
The family is scatter'd yet,
    Though of one home and heart ;
Part militant in earthly gloom,
    In heavenly glory part.

But who can speak the rapture, when
The number is complete,
And all the children sunder'd now,
Around one Father meet ?
One fold, one Shepherd, one employ,
One everlasting Home :
" Lo ! I come quickly : " Even so ;
Amen ! Lord Jesus, come.

ATHANASIUS.

ATHANASIUS CONTRA MUNDUM.

THE world against me, I against the
    world :
Strange words for him who just now
    stood
On Alexandria's throne and hurled
    His thunders as he would.
But rock is not less rock, though forced at last
    To fall before the beating sea ;
Nor may I be the less myself though cast
    Away from majesty.

God's truth I stand on, can I need a throne ?
    Or bishop's vesture, if I feel
His mercy wrap me with a warmth its own,
    While at His feet I kneel ?
No, let them drive me thrice again from sway,
    As they, ere-this, three times have driven,
So but the Lord be at my side alway,
    I will deem exile heaven.

They call me haughty, of opinion proud,
 Untaught to bend a stubborn will ;
Ah little dreams the shallow-hearted crowd
 What thoughts this bosom fill,
What loneliness this outer strength doth hide,
 What longing lies beneath this calm,
For human sympathy so long untried,
 Our earth's divinest balm.

But more than sympathy the truth I prize ;
 Above my friendships hold I God,
And stricken be these feet ere they despise
 The path their Master trod.
So let my banner be again unfurled,
 Again its cheerless motto seen,
"The world against me, I against the world : "
 Judge Thou, dear Christ, between.

The Forgiveness of Sins.

FAITH.

FAITH is a very slender thing,
    Though little understood;
    It frees the soul from death's dread sting,
By resting in the Blood.

It looks not on the things around,
    Nor on the things within;
It takes its flight to scenes above,
    Beyond the spheres of sin.

It sees, upon the throne of God,
    A Victim that was slain;
It rests its all on His shed blood,
    And says, I'm born again.

Faith is not what we feel or see;
    It is a simple trust

In what the God of Love has said
 Of Jesus, as " the Just."

The Perfect One, that died for me,
 Upon His Father's throne
Presents our names before our God,
 And pleads Himself alone.

What Jesus is, and that alone,
 Is faith's delightful plea ;
It never deals with sinful self,
 Or righteous self, in me.

It tells me I am counted " dead "
 By God, in His own Word ;
It tells me I am born again
 In Christ, my risen Lord.

In that He died, He died to sin ;
 In that He lives — to God ;
'Then I am dead to nature's hopes,
 And justified through blood.

If He is free, then I am free
 From all unrighteousness ;

If He is just, then I am just :
  He is my Righteousness.

What want I more to perfect bliss ?
  A body like His own
Will perfect me for greater joys
  Than angels' round the Throne.

SHE HATH DONE WHAT SHE COULD.

SHE brought her box of alabaster,
  The precious spikenard filled the room
With honor worthy of the Master,
A costly, rare, and rich perfume.

Her tears for sin fell hot and thickly
  On His dear feet, outstretcht and bare ;
Unconscious how, she wiped them quickly
  With the long ringlets of her hair.

And richly fall those raven tresses
  Adown her cheek, like willow-leaves,
As stooping still, with fond caresses,
  She plies her task of love, and grieves.

Oh may we thus, like loving Mary,
  Ever our choicest offerings bring,
Nor grudging of our toil, nor chary
  Of costly service to our King.

Methinks I hear from Christian lowly
  Some hallowed voice at evening rise,

Or quiet morn, or in the holy,
    Unclouded calm of Sabbath skies, —

I bring my box of alabaster,
    Of earthly loves I break the shrine,
And pour affections, purer, vaster,
    On that dear Head, those feet of Thine.

The joys I prized, the hopes I cherisht,
    The fairest flowers my fancy wove,
Behold my fondest idols perisht,
    Receive the incense of my love !

What though the scornful world, deriding
    Such waste of love, of service, fears,
Still let me pour, through taunt and chiding,
    The rich libation of my tears.

I bring my box of alabaster, —
    Accepted let the offering rise !
So grateful tears shall flow the faster,
    In founts of gladness, from my eyes !

BEHOLD, I STAND AT THE DOOR AND KNOCK.

IN the silent midnight watches
    List — thy bosom door !
How it knocketh, knocketh, knocketh,
  Knocketh evermore !
Say not 't is thy pulse's beating :
    'T is thy heart of sin ;
'T is thy Saviour knocks, and crieth,
    " Rise and let Me in."

Death comes on with reckless footsteps
    To the hall and hut ;
Think you Death will tarry, knocking,
    When the door is shut ?
Jesus waiteth, waiteth, waiteth,
    But the door is fast ;
Grieved, away thy Saviour goeth,
    Death breaks in at last.

Then 't is time to stand entreating
    Christ to let thee in ;

At the gate of Heaven beating,
    Wailing for thy sin.
Nay, alas ! thou guilty creature,
    Hast thou, then, forgot ?
Jesus waited long to know thee,
    Now He knows thee not.

15

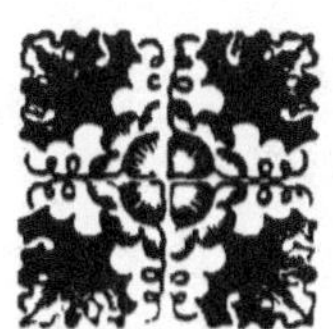

THE SUN OF RIGHTEOUSNESS.

" But unto you that fear my Name shall the Sun of Righteousness arise with healing in His wings."— MAI. iv. 2.

THE sick man in his chamber,
　　Through the long, weary night
　　Tossed on his restless pillow,
How longs he for the light!

He counts the hours that linger,
　　Heavy with clouds and rain,
And a great weight of darkness
　　Lies on his fevered brain.

He hears the loud clock ticking,
　　And the owl hoot afar;
While glimmers the pale night-light,
　　And fades the midnight star;

Till eastward in the Heaven
　　He sees at last the sign, —
O'er the far purple mountain
　　A single silver line.

It broadens and it deepens
　To a sea of red and gold,
With clouds of rosy amber
　Around its glory rolled.

Till each pane of his window
　Is silvered o'er and o'er,
And lines of golden arrows
　Lie on the dusky floor.

The sick soul lieth weary
　In the world's soft unrest,
With clouds of care and sorrow
　And weight of sins opprest.

Out of the night she crieth,
　Out of the narrow room :
O Saviour, gentle Saviour,
　Wilt Thou not pierce the gloom ?

Break on this night of longing,
　Where hand in hand we grope,
Through wastes of vain endeavor,
　'Neath stars of fruitless hope.

O'er the great hills of sadness
　That hem us darkly in,

Rough with our tears and losses,
  And black with many a sin ; —

Rise, rise above the mountains,
  With healing on Thy wings ;
Break, break into the chambers,
  Where pain in secret stings.

Come while the morning tarries,
  Our waiting eyes to bless ;
Look through the lowly lattice,
  Bright Sun of Righteousness !

Set for the hearts that love Thee
  Thy token up above, —
The white rays of redemption,
  And the red fire of love.

Out of our gloom we call Thee,
  Out of our helpless night ;
Sun of the world, sweet Saviour,
  Show us 'Thy perfect light.

THE WANDERER.

*" I have gone astray like a sheep that is lost : O seek
Thy servant ; for I do not forget Thy commandments."*

FAR from the Shepherd's one true Fold
    I stray,
In pathways all unknown ;
O dark and gloomy is the woful day
    That finds me here alone.

My hopes are blighted and my heart bereft
    Of comfort and repose,
Because the Shepherd's blessed Fold I left,
    To wander where I chose.

I sought more liberty and less restraint ;
    My will I wished to please ;
And all day long I made a vain complaint,
    For greater rest and ease ;

At last I broke away and left the flock,
    To find a desert bare —
No food, no cooling stream, no sheltering
    rock, —
    False dreams and blank despair.

Oh for the Fold, the blessed Fold once more !
       Oh for the Shepherd's hand,
To guide me back, and lead me as of yore
       In verdant pasture land !

Oh seek me, tender Shepherd, lest I die ;
       Find me and take me home ;
Once there again in calm security,
       My feet shall never roam.

Thy staff may strike, — I will not shrink again,
       Or spurn Thy warning voice,
Or seek a pathway without toil or pain,
       Of mine own erring choice.

But in the footsteps of the flock my way
       With duteous love I 'll take,
And strive to curb my will, and day by day
       All devious ways forsake.

Then seek me, tender Shepherd, lest I die,
       Or further from Thee roam ;
In pity heed Thy wanderer's heart-wrung cry,
       And bring me safely home.

"WHO CAN FORGIVE SINS, BUT GOD ONLY?"

ONE Priest alone can pardon me,
   Or bid me " Go in peace ; "
   Can breathe that word, " Absolvo te,"
And make these heart-throbs cease :
My soul hath heard His priestly voice ;
It said, " I bore thy sins, — rejoice ! "

He show'd the spear-mark in His side,
   The nail-print on His palm ;
Said, " Look on Me, the crucified ;
   Why tremble thus ?   Be calm !
All power is mine — I set thee free, —
Be not afraid — Absolvo te."

By Him my soul is purified,
   Once leprous and defiled,
Cleansed in the fountain from His side,
   God sees me as a child :
No priest can heal or cleanse but He ;
No other say, " Absolvo te."

He robed me in a priestly dress
  That I might incense bring,
Of prayer and praise and righteousness,
  To heaven's eternal King :
And when He gave this robe to me,
He smiled and said, " Absolvo te."

In heaven He stands before the throne,
  The great High-Priest above,
" Melchisedec," — that name alone
  Can sin's dark stain remove :
To Him I look on bended knee,
And hear that sweet — " Absolvo te."

A girded Levite here below,
  I willing service bring,
And fain would tell to all I know
  Of Christ, the Priestly King :
Would win all hearts from sin to flee,
And hear Him say, " Absolvo te."

A little while, and He shall come
  Forth from the inner shrine,
To call His pardon'd brethren home ;
O bliss, supreme, divine !
When every blood-bought child shall see
The Priest who said, " Absolvo te."

KYRIE ELEISON.

LORD Jesus Christ, my faithful Shep-
    herd, hear ;
  Feed me with Thy grace, draw inly
    near ;
By Thee redeem'd, in Thee alone I live,
All I need 't is Thou canst give :
        Kyrie Eleison.

Ah, Lord, Thy timid sheep now feed
With joy upon Thy heavenly mead,
  Lead us to the crystal river
  Whence our life is flowing ever :
        Kyrie Eleison.

For Thou art calling all the toil-oppress'd,
All the weary to Thy rest ;
  The pardon of their sins is here bestow'd,
  Thou dost free them from their load :
        Kyrie Eleison.

Ah, come, Thyself put forth Thine hand,
Unbind this heavy iron band,
 Set me from my sorrows free,
 Give me strength to follow Thee :
    Kyrie Eleison.

Thou fain wouldst heart and Soul to Thee incline,
Take me from myself and make me Thine ;
 Thou art the Vine and I the branch, oh, grant
 I may grow a living plant :
    Kyrie Eleison.

For nought but sin I find in me,
Yet are they done away in Thee ;
 Mine are anguish, fear, unrest,
 But in Thee, Lord, I am blest :
    Kyrie Eleison.

The Resurrection of the Body.

I BELIEVE IN THE RESURRECTION OF THE BODY.

DEAR Saviour of a dying world,
　　Where grief and change must be,
　　In the new grave where Thou wast laid,
　My heart lies down with Thee.
Oh, not in cold despair of joy,
　Or weariness of pain,
But from a hope that shall not die,
　To rise and live again.

I would arise in all Thy strength
　My place on earth to fill,
To work out all my time of war
　With love's unflinching will ;
Firm against every doubt of Thee
　For all my future way —
To walk in Heaven's eternal light
　Throughout the changing day.

Ah, such a day as thou shalt own.
    When suns have ceased to shine !
A day of burdens borne by Thee,
    And work that all was Thine.
Speed Thy bright rising in my heart,
    Thy righteous kingdom speed, —
Till my whole life in concord say,
    " The Lord is risen indeed."

Oh for an impulse from Thy love
    With every coming breath,
To sing that sweet undying song
    Amid the wrecks of death !
A " hail ! " to every mortal pang
    That bids me take my right
To glory in the blessed life
    Which Thou hast brought to light.

I long to see the hallowed earth
    In new creation rise, —
To find the germs of Eden hid
    Where its fallen beauty lies, —
To feel the spring-tide of a soul
    By one deep love set free ;
Made meet to lay aside her dust,
    And be at home with Thee.

And then — there shall be yet an end —
　An end how full to bless!
How dear to those who watch for Thee
　With human tenderness!
Then shall the saying come to pass
　That makes our home complete,
And, rising from the conquered grave,
　Thy parted ones shall meet.

Yes — they shall meet, and face to face
　By heart to heart be known,
Clothed with Thy likeness, Lord of life,
　And perfect in their own.
For this corruptible must rise,
　From its corruption free,
And this frail mortal must put on
　Thine immortality.

Shine, then, Thou Resurrection Light,
　Upon our sorrows shine!
The fulness of Thy joy be ours,
　As all our griefs were Thine.
Now, in this changing, dying life
　Our faded hopes restore,
Till, in Thy triumph perfected,
　We taste of death no more.

THE WIDOW OF NAIN.

"And when the Lord saw her, He had compassion on her, and said unto her, Weep not." — LUKE vii. 13.

FORTH from the city gate,
   As evening shadows lengthen o'er the
      plain,
And the hushed crowd in reverent silence
      wait,
   Passed out a funeral train.

Only one mourner there,
Slowly, with feeble steps, following the dead,
In the sad travail of the soul's despair
   Bowed down her stricken head.

For him she wept forlorn,
Of care the solace, and of age the stay,
Whose silver cord was broken ere the morn
   Had brightened into day.

Thus hath it ever been, —
Time, the destroyer, sweeps relentless by,

When hopes are strong and leaves of promise
      green,
And manhood's heart beats high.

Who comes of stately mien,
As one with travel weary, seeking rest, —
Whose aspect gentle, and whose brow serene,
      Speak of a mission blest?

'T is He, with power to save,
Who where desponding grief his vigil kept,
Knowing all human sufferings, at the grave
      Of Lazarus wept.

Thus spake He, — "Weep no more!
Be still, sad heart!   Be dry, ye moistened eyes!
Thus to the living I the dead restore!
      Sleeper, awake, arise!"

Then at His bidding came
To those cold lips the warm, returning breath;
Then did He kindle life's extinguished flame,
      Victor o'er Sin and Death.

And thus He ever stands, —
Friend of the fallen, wiping all tears away,

Wherever Sorrow lifts her suppliant hands,
     And Faith remains to pray.

     Where'er the wretched flee,
From the rude conflict of this world distrest,
Consoling words He whispers, — " Come to Me,
     And I will give you rest!"

     'Till at the second birth,
He bids the woes and wrongs of ages cease,
And brings to an emancipated earth,
     Judgment, and truth, and peace ;

     And gathers all His own
From the four winds to that eternal shore,
Where Mercy sits upon the great white throne,
     And Death shall be no more.

THE GRAVE AT BETHANY.

LOVE'S tears fell fast, like the thick rain
that weepeth
    Earth's glory fled ;
" She goeth to the grave," they said, " she
keepeth
    Watch o'er the dead."

But she hath heard the Master's call, and goeth
    Her Lord to meet ;
Her bursting heart with her pale form she
throweth
    Low at His feet.

" Hadst *Thou* been here ! " — Faith's trembling
sunbeam glistens
    Through sorrow's cloud :
Touched with the feeling of her tears, He listens
    In anguish bowed.

" Hadst *Thou* been here ! " — Like gloom the
land o'ershading,
    Where sunshine slept,
16

Came o'er His Godlike soul that soft upbraiding,
    And Jesus wept.

"Where have ye laid him?"—Where the cypress clinging
    Skirts the low cave,
He stands, a light o'er Death's dark empire flinging,
    Mighty to save.

Hushed are all sounds, while like soft mists ascending,
    Quiet and calm,
Goes up to Heaven the solemn prayer, portending
    Grief's richest balm.

"Lazarus, come forth!"—Far down in death's abysses
    The glad soul heard,
And, like a babe new waked by morning kisses,
    To life is stirred;

And as a dream one waking moment tarries,
    Then melts in night,
No thought of those dark days the spirit carries
    Back to the light;

But even as one who some brief while hath
       wandered
         On field or foam,
And still on loved ones left each night hath
       pondered,
         Yearning for home,—

He comes again—all sweet familiar faces
         Beholds once more;
Each natural scene the foreign past displaces
         From memory's store;—

So, without painful change, or fearful wonder,
         From his calm bed,
Parting the curtains of the grave asunder,
         Came forth the Dead;

Earnest of that far time, when, to us waking,
         This life shall seem,
Amid that higher Life upon us breaking,
         A strange, faint dream.

THE MAID IS NOT DEAD, BUT SLEEPETH.

LEFT in her little room alone,
　　The Ruler's child lay stiff and dead,
　　While, vainly warm, the Syrian sun
Play'd round her cold and silent bed;

While, vainly soft, from Judah's hills
　　Sigh'd through the lattice the soft air,
That could not move the close white lip,
　　Nor heave again the bosom fair.

The voice of anguish and despair
　　Is loud within the chamber near,
Of them lamenting bitterly
　　Her early doom with groan and tear.

Her mother maketh grievous moan :—
　　" Ah ! had the sire more swiftly sped,
And brought the mighty Prophet here
　　Ere the last lingering breath was fled !

" What now avails that far away
    Comes o'er the plain his hastening tread !
Go tell him that he trouble not
    The Master more ; my child is dead."

Dead ! is all o'er when that is said ?
    Are hope, and trust, and comfort, gone ?
The servant tells the weeping sire,
    And yet the Prophet journeys on.

He stands amid the mourning throng :
    " Why do ye make this bitter cry ?
The damsel is not dead, she sleeps."
    They laugh in scorn, — they saw her die.

Yea, but they see not the strong power
    For life and death that standeth by,
Nor read the awful Godhead veil'd
    Beneath that meekly patient eye.

Go forth, then, unbelieving throng ;
    The three apostles, and the twain
Who love so tenderly, alone
    Shall see her spirit come again.

Now waken, waken, little maiden,
    His foot is on thy chamber-floor,

The Lord God of the living cometh
  Thine earthly being to restore.

He takes her cold resistless hand : —
  " Damsel, I say to thee, arise."
Lo, life returns, with mantling flow,
  To cheek, and brow, and kindling eyes.

She riseth up, she walketh forth,
  Her lip is red, her heart is warm ;
He gives her to her mother's kiss,
  He gives her to her father's arm.

Surely, we too have hope in sorrow,
  Who for our Christian brethren weep ;
Christ is our Life and Resurrection ;
  They are not dead, they do but sleep.

And the Life Everlasting.

STRANGERS AND SOJOURNERS.

WE have no home on earth below,
　　And time is short and heaven is near;
　O that our hearts were weanèd so
That we could live like strangers here:

Like pilgrims that have paused an hour
　　To rest upon some foreign strand ;
Like banished men that love to pour
　　The praises of their Fatherland !

Bright are the flowers that God has lent
　　To bloom beneath the traveller's tread ;
And beautiful the starry tent
　　He spreadeth o'er the pilgrim's head.

But in the Land that 's far away
　　There needs no light of sun or moon ;
And flowers that never know decay
　　Along its starless shores are strewn.

BELOW AND ABOVE.

DOWN below the wild November whist-
　　ling
　　Through the beech's dome of burning
　　red,
And the Autumn sprinkling penitential
　　Dust and ashes on the chestnut's head.

Down below a pall of airy purple,
　　Darkly hanging from the mountain-side,
And the sunset from his eyebrow staring
　　O'er the long roll of the leaden tide.

Up above the Tree with leaf unfading,
　　By the everlasting river's brink,
And the Sea of glass, beyond whose margin
　　Never yet the sun was known to sink.

Down below the white wings of the sea-bird,
　　Dashed across the furrows dark with mould,
Flitting like the memories of our childhood
　　Through the trees now waxen pale and old.

Down below imaginations quivering
   Through our human spirits like the wind,
Thoughts that toss like leaves about the wood-
      land,
   Hopes like sea-birds flashed across the mind.

Up above the host no man can number,
   In white robes, a palm in every hand,
Each some work sublime forever working,
   In the spacious tracts of that great Land.

Up above the thoughts that know not anguish,
   Tender care, sweet love for us below,
Noble pity free from anxious terror,
   Larger love without a touch of woe.

Down below a sad, mysterious music,
   Wailing through the woods and on the shore,
Burdened with a grand majestic secret
   That keeps sweeping from us evermore.

Up above a music that entwineth,
   With eternal threads of golden sound,
The great poem of this strange existence,
   All whose wondrous meaning hath been
      found.

Down below the Church to whose poor win-
          dow
    Glory by the autumnal trees is lent,
And a knot of worshippers in mourning,
    Missing some one at the Sacrament.

Up above the burst of Hallelujah,
    And (without the sacramental mist
Wrapt around us like a sunlit halo)
    The great vision of the face of Christ.

Down below cold sunlight on the tombstones,
    And the green, wet turf with faded flowers,
Winter roses, once like young hopes burning,
    Now beneath the ivy dripped with showers :

And the new-made grave within the church-
          yard,
    And the white cap on that young face pale,
And the watcher ever as it dusketh
    Rocking to and fro with that long wail.

Up above a crowned and happy spirit,
    Like an infant in the eternal years,
Who shall grow in love and light forever,
    Ordered in his place among his peers.

Oh the sobbing of the winds of autumn,
  Oh the sunset streak of stormy gold,
Oh the poor heart thinking in the church-yard,
  " Night is coming, and the grave is cold."

Oh the pale and plashed and sodden roses,
  Oh the desolate heart that grave above,
Oh the white cap shaking as it darkens
  Round that shrine of memory and love.

Oh the rest forever, and the rapture !
  Oh the Hand that wipes the tears away !
Oh the golden homes beyond the sunset,
  And the hope that watches o'er the clay !

NOW IS OUR SALVATION NEARER THAN WHEN WE BELIEVED.

ONE sweetly solemn thought
    Comes to me o'er and o'er, —
I 'm nearer home to-day
Than I ever have been before."

Nearer my Father's House,
    Where the many mansions be,
Nearer the Great White Throne,
    Nearer the Jasper Sea ;

Nearer the bound of life,
    Where we lay our burdens down,
Nearer leaving the Cross,
    Nearer gaining the Crown.

But lying darkly between,
    Winding down through the night,
Is the dim and unknown stream
    That leads me at last to the Light.

Closer, closer my steps
  Come to the dark abysm,
Closer Death to my lips
  Presses the awful chrysm.

Saviour, perfect my trust,
  Strengthen the might of my faith;
Let me feel as I would when I stand
  On the rock of the shore of death;—

Feel as I would when my feet
  Are slipping over the brink,
For it may be I'm nearer Home—
  Nearer now than I think!

THE DEATH OF THE CHRISTIAN.

ACTS XII.

THE Apostle slept, — a light shone in
    the prison,
  An angel touched his side ;
" Arise ! " he said ; and quickly he hath risen,
  His fettered arms untied.

The watchers saw no light at midnight gleaming,
  They heard no sound of feet ;
The gates fly open, and the saint, still dreaming,
  Stands free upon the street.

So when the Christian's eyelid droops and closes
  In nature's parting strife,
A friendly Angel stands where he reposes,
  To wake him up to life.

He gives a gentle blow, and so releases
  The spirit from its clay ;
From sin's temptations, and from life's distresses,
  He bids it come away.

It rises up, and from its darksome mansion
  It takes its silent flight ;
And feels its freedom in the large expansion
  Of heavenly air and light.

Behind, it hears Time's iron gates close faintly,
  It now is far from them ;
For it has reached the City of the saintly,
  The New Jerusalem.

A voice is heard on earth of kinsfolk weeping
  The loss of one they love :
But he is gone where the redeemed are keeping
  A Festival above !

The mourners throng the way, and from the
      steeple
  The funeral-bell tolls slow ;
But on the golden streets the holy people
  Are passing to and fro ;

And saying as they meet, " Rejoice ! another,
  Long waited for, is come ;"
The Saviour's heart is glad, a younger brother
  Hath reached the Father's Home !

WHO, AND WHENCE?

NOT from Jerusalem alone
   To heaven the path ascends ;
      As near, as sure, as straight the way
  That leads to the celestial day,
 From furthest realms extends —
From furthest realms extends —
Frigid or torrid zone.

What matters how or when we start ?
   One is the crown to all ;
      One is the hard but glorious race,
      Whatever be our starting-place ;
  Rings round the earth the call
That says, Arise, depart !

From the balm-breathing, sun-loved isles
   Of the bright Southern sea,
      From the dead North's cloud-shadowed
        pole,
      We gather to one gladsome goal,—
  One common home in thee,
City of sun and smiles !

The cold, rough billow hinders none ;
  Nor helps the calm, fair main ;
    The brown rock of Norwegian gloom,
    The verdure of Tahitian bloom,
  The sands of Misriam's plain,
Or peaks of Lebanon.

As from the green lands of the vine,
  So from the snow wastes pale,
    We find the ever-open road
    To the dear city of our God ;
  From Russian steppe, or Burman vale,
Or terraced Palestine.

Not from swift Jordan's sacred stream
  Alone we mount above ;
    Indus or Danube, Thames or Rhone,
    Rivers unsainted and unknown,
  From each the Home of love
Beckons with heavenly gleam.

Not from gray Olivet alone
  We see the gates of life ;
    From Morven's heath or Jungfrau's snow,
    We welcome the descending glow
  Of pearl and chrysolite,
And the unsetting sun.

17

Not from Jerusalem alone
  The Church ascends to God ;
    Strangers of every tongue and clime,
    Pilgrims of every land and time,
  Throng the well-trodden road
That leads up to the throne.

ONLY WAITING.

ONLY waiting till the shadows
　　Are a little longer grown ;
　Only waiting till the glimmer
Of the day's last beam is flown ;
Till the night of earth is faded
　From the heart once full of day ;.
Till the stars of heaven are breaking
　Through the twilight, soft and gray.

Only waiting till the reapers
　Have the last sheaf gathered home ;
For the summer time is faded,
　And the autumn winds have come ;
Quickly, reapers ! gather quickly
　These last ripe hours of my heart,
For the bloom of life is withered,
　And I hasten to depart.

Only waiting till the angels
　Open wide the mystic gate,
At whose feet I long have lingered,
　Weary, poor, and desolate.

Even now I hear their footsteps
  And their voices far away ;
If they call me, I am waiting, —
  Only waiting to obey.

Only waiting till the shadows
  Are a little longer grown ;
Only waiting till the glimmer
  Of the day's last beam is flown :
Then from out the gathering darkness
  Holy, deathless stars shall rise,
By whose light my soul shall gladly
  Tread its pathway to the skies !

GOING HOME.

"Suffer the little children to come unto Me, and forbid them not: for of such is the kingdom of God." — ST. MARK X. 14.

THEY are going — only going —
 Jesus called them long ago;
All the wintry time they're pass-
 ing
Softly as the falling snow.
When the violets in the spring-time
 Catch the azure of the sky,
They are carried out to slumber
 Sweetly where the violets lie.

They are going — only going —
 When with summer earth is drest,
In their cold hands holding roses
 Folded to each silent breast:
When the autumn hangs red banners
 Out above the harvest sheaves,
They are going — ever going —
 Thick and fast, like falling leaves.

All along the mighty ages,
    All adown the solemn time,
They have taken up their homeward
    March to that serener clime,
Where the watching, waiting Angels
    Lead them from the shadow dim,
To the brightness of His presence
    Who has called them unto Him.

They are going — only going —
    Out of pain and into bliss ;
Out of sad and sinful weakness
    Into perfect holiness.
Snowy brows — no care shall shade them ;
    Bright eyes — tears shall never dim ;
Rosy lips — no time shall fade them ;
    Jesus called them unto Him.

Little hearts for ever stainless, —
    Little hands as pure as they, —
Little feet, by Angels guided,
    Never a forbidden way!
They are going — ever going —
    Leaving many a lonely spot ;
But 't is Jesus who has called them —
    Suffer, and forbid them not !

THE JERUSALEM THAT IS ABOVE.

BRIEF life is here our portion ;
 Brief sorrow, short-lived care ;
The life that knows no ending,
 The tearless life, is *there.*

O happy retribution !
 Short toil, eternal rest :
For mortals and for sinners
 A mansion with the blest.

And now we fight the battle,
 But then shall wear the crown
Of full and everlasting
 And passionless renown :

And now we watch and struggle,
 And now we live in hope,
And Sion in her anguish
 With Babylon must cope :

But He whom now we trust in
 Shall then be seen and known ;

And they that know and see Him
 Shall have Him for their own.

The morning shall awaken,
 The shadows flee away,
And each true-hearted servant
 Shall shine as doth the day.

There God, our King and Portion,
 In fulness of His grace,
Shall we behold forever,
 And worship face to face.

Part II.

For thee, O dear, dear Country,
 Mine eyes their vigils keep ;
For very love, beholding
 Thy happy name, they weep.

The mention of thy glory
 Is unction to the breast,
And medicine in sickness,
 And love, and light, and rest.

O one, O only Mansion !
 O Paradise of Joy !

Where tears are ever banished,
　And smiles have no alloy ;

The Lamb is all thy splendor,
　The Crucified thy praise ;
His laud and benediction
　Thy ransomed people raise.

With Jasper glow thy bulwarks,
　Thy streets with emeralds blaze ;
The sardius and the topaz
　Unite in thee their rays ;

Thine ageless walls are bonded
　With amethyst unpriced ;
The saints build up its fabric,
　And the corner-stone is Christ.

Thou hast no shore, fair ocean !
　Thou hast no time, bright day !
Dear fountain of refreshment
　To pilgrims far away !

Upon the Rock of Ages
　They raise thy holy tower ;
Thine is the victor's laurel,
　And thine the golden dower.

PART III.

Jerusalem the golden !
  With milk and honey blest !
Beneath thy contemplation
  Sink heart and voice opprest.

I know not, oh ! I know not
  What joys await us there ;
What radiancy of glory,
  What bliss beyond compare.

They stand, those halls of Sion,
  All jubilant with song,
And bright with many an Angel,
  And all the martyr throng :

The Prince is ever in them,
  The daylight ever bright ;
The pastures of the blessed
  Are decked in glorious light.

There is a throne of David ;
  And there, from care released,
The shout of them that triumph,
  The song of them that feast ;

And they, who with their Leader.
  Have conquered in the fight,
For ever and for ever
  Are clad in robes of white.

O sweet and blessed Country,
  The Home of God's elect!
O sweet and blessed Country,
  That eager hearts expect !

Jesu, in mercy bring us
  To that dear land of rest :
Who art, with God the Father,
  And Spirit, ever blest.

NO NIGHT THERE.

THERE is no night in heaven:
    In that blest world above
    Work never can bring weariness,
For work itself is love.
There is no night in heaven:
Yet nightly round the bed
Of every Christian wanderer
    Faith hears an angel tread.

    There is no grief in heaven:
    For life is one glad day,
And tears are of those former things
    Which all have passed away.
    There is no grief in heaven:
    Yet angels from on high
On golden pinions earthward glide,
    The Christian's tears to dry.

There is no sin in heaven :
Behold that blessed throng ;
All holy is their spotless robe,
All holy is their song.
There is no sin in heaven :
Here who from sin is free ?
Yet angels aid us in our strife
For Christ's true liberty.

There is no death in heaven :
For they who gain that shore
Have won their immortality,
And they can die no more.
There is no death in heaven :
But when the Christian dies,
The angels 'wait his parted soul,
And waft it to the skies.

"THOU ART MY PORTION, O LORD!"

I HAVE a heritage of joy
    That yet I must not see,
The hand that bled to make it mine
Is keeping it for me.

I have a certainty of love
    That sets my heart at rest,
A calm assurance for to-day,
    That to·be thus is best.

My heart is resting, O my God,
    My heart is in Thy care;
I hear the voice of joy and health
    Resounding everywhere.

" Thou art my portion," saith my soul—
    " Amen!" sweet voices say;
The music of that glad Amen
    Will never die away.

" TILL THE CHANGE COME."

THE SONG OF DOUBT.

THIS earth is the court of a palace,
  Where petitioners wait for the King,
  Till the solemn-eyed servitor cometh
Them into the Presence to bring.
Till Death, the dread summoner, cometh,
  While with fear all the waiters are dumb,
And he beckoneth, beckoneth ever,
  Saying, " Up ! for thy hour is come."
Saying, " Up ! for thy waiting is ended."
  Then dismally brazen bells swing,
And sad with a gloomy foreboding,
  We go to the Court of the King.

THE SONG OF FAITH.

This earth is watching and waiting,
  Looking on and longing by night,
While far on the distant horizon,
  The heavens are belted with light—

The heavens are bright at His coming,
　Who bringeth the message of love,
And who beckoneth, beckoneth ever,
　Saying, "Come to thy Father above."
Saying, "Come! for the King is thy Father."
　Then sweetly the happy bells ring,
And gladly with hearts of rejoicing,
　We go to the Court of the King.

Oro.

18

THE MOUNT OF OLIVES.

*" He went out into a mountain to pray, and continued
all night in prayer to God."* — LUKE vi. 12.

THOU didst love the evening hours,
　　Saviour of the world and me,
　　And the closing of the flowers
Brought a welcome rest to Thee,
As the hireling gladly sees
The long shadows of the trees.

Rest, but not on beds of down,
　　Curtained close in soft repose ;
Thou didst seek the mountain's crown ;
　　Where the shady olive grows,
Thou didst find a place of prayer,
Commune with Thy Father there.

Ah ! methinks I see Thee now,
　　Climbing, late, the mountain-side ;
Cool night breezes fan Thy brow,
　　Day's long cares in shadows hide :
Far below the Eastern steep
Salem lies in double sleep !

All day long those hands of Thine
 Mercy's almoners have been;
All day long those eyes Divine
 Sights of want and woe have seen;
All day long those ears have heard
Many a harsh and sinful word.

Angel hands Thy couch shall spread
 On the green and mossy sward;
At Thy feet and at Thy head
 Cherubs shall keep watch and ward:
Bright, like his at Luz, shall be
Midnight visions unto Thee!

Nay, He rests not,—see Him there,
 Kneeling low upon the sod,
All the burden of His prayer
 Pouring forth as man to God;
Far away from earthly jars,
In the clear, calm light of stars.

For Himself He prays awhile,—
 Strength to do His will on earth;
He whose spirit knew no guile,
 Bore no taint of sinful birth,—
Strength to bear His Father's frown,
Grace to spurn the proffered crown:

Then for those few simple sheep,
  Earnest of His future Fold,
Fervent yearnings upward leap,
  Faith and Hope for them grow bold ;
Angel censers through the air
Waft the perfume of His prayer.

But the first gray light of morning
  Pierces now the olive shade ;
Early birds, with gentle warning,
  Carol through the leafy glade ;
All unrested, save by prayer,
Jesus drinks the morning air.

Saviour ! let the evening hours
  Dear to us, Thy children, be ;
With clasped hands, as folded flowers,
  Praying earnestly to Thee,
Let our vesper-worship rise
Incense-like before Thine eyes ;—

Then, when that dark eventide
  Closes in our life's long day,
And, like some steep mountain-side,
  Frowns the last and lonesome way,
Bright to us that path shall be,
Found alone, O Lord, with Thee !

A PRAYER.

ASK not wealth, but power to take
   And use the things I have aright ;
Not years, but wisdom that shall make
My life a profit and delight.

I ask not that for me the plan
   Of good and ill be set aside,
But that the common lot of man
   Be nobly borne and glorified.

I know I may not always keep
   My steps in places green and sweet,
Nor find the pathway of the deep
   A path of safety to my feet.

But pray, that, when the tempest's breath
   Shall fiercely sweep my way about,
I make not shipwreck of my faith
   In the unbottomed sea of doubt ;

And that, though it be mine to know
   How hard the stoniest pillow seems,

Good angels still may come and go
  On the bright ladder of my dreams.

I do not ask for love below,—
  That friends shall never be estranged ;
But for the power of loving, so
  My heart may keep its youth unchanged.

Youth, joy, wealth — Fate, I give thee these :
  Leave faith and hope till life is passed ;
And leave my heart's best impulses
  Fresh and unfailing to the last.

For this I count, of all sweet things,
  The sweetest out of heaven above ;
And loving others surely brings
  The fullest recompense of love !

REST AND PEACE IN TRUTH.

 DO not ask, O Lord, that Thou
    shouldst shed
Full radiance here ;
Give but a ray of peace, that I may tread
    Without a fear ;
I do not ask my cross to understand,
    My way to see —
Better in darkness just to feel Thy hand
    And follow Thee.
Joy is like restless day ; but peace divine,
    Like quiet night :
Lead me, O Lord — till perfect day shall shine,
    Through peace to light.

HERE IS MY HEART.

HERE is my heart!—my God, I give it
Thee;
I heard Thee call and say,
" Not to the world, my child, but unto me ;"—
I heard and will obey.
Here is love's offering to my King,
Which in glad sacrifice I bring, —
Here is my heart!

Here is my heart!—surely the gift, though poor,
My God will not despise;
Vainly and long I sought to make it pure,
To meet Thy searching eyes ;
Corrupted once in Adam's fall,
The stains of sin pollute it all, —
My guilty heart!

Here is my heart!—my heart so sad before,
Now by Thy grace made meet ;
Yet bruised and wearied, it can only pour
Its anguish at Thy feet ;

It groans beneath the weight of sin,
　It sighs salvation's joy to win, —
　　　My mourning heart!

Here is my heart! — in Christ its longings end,
　Near to the cross it draws;
It says, " Thou art my portion, O, my Friend!
　Thy blood my ransom was."
And in the Saviour it has found
　What blessedness and peace abound, —
　　　My trusting heart!

Here is my heart! — ah! Holy Spirit, come,
　Its nature to renew,
And consecrate it wholly as Thy home,
　A temple fair and true.
Teach it to love and serve Thee more,
　To fear Thee, trust Thee, and adore, —
　　　My cleansed heart!

Here is my heart! — it trembles to draw near
　The glory of Thy throne:
Give it the shining robe Thy servants wear,
　Of righteousness Thine own;
Its pride and folly chase away,
　Thou who art wise, and just, and true, —
　　　My waiting heart!

Here is my heart! — O Friend of friends, be near
  To make the tempter fly;
And when my latest foe I wait with fear,
  Give me the victory.
Gladly on Thy love reposing,
  Let me say, when life is closing,
      "Here is my heart!"

A SOUL'S ENTREATY.

LORD, what unvalued pleasures crowned
　　The days of old !
　When Thou wert so familiar found,
Those days were gold.

When Abram wished, Thou couldst afford
　　With him to feast ;
When Lot but said, " Turn in, my Lord,"
　　Thou wert his guest.

But ah ! this heart of mine doth pant
　　And beat for Thee,
Yet Thou art strange, and wilt not grant
　　Thyself to me.

What ! shall Thy people be so dear
　　To Thee no more ?
Or is not heaven to earth so near
　　As heretofore ?

The famished raven's hoarser cry
    Finds out Thine ear ;
My soul is famished, and I die,
    Except Thou hear.

O Thou great Alpha ! King of kings !
    Or bow to me,
Or lend my soul seraphic wings
    To mount to Thee.

EVENING HYMN OF THE GREEKS.

HE day is past and over ;
　　All thanks, O Lord, to Thee !
　I pray Thee that offenceless
The hours of dark may be.
O Jesu, keep me in Thy sight,
And save me through the coming night !

　Lighten mine eyes, O Saviour,
　　Or sleep in death shall I ;
　And he, my wakeful Tempter,
　　Triumphantly shall cry :
" He could not make their darkness light,
Nor guard them through the hours of night ! "

　Be Thou my soul's preserver,
　　O God, for Thou dost know
　How many are the perils
　　Through which I have to go :
Lover of men ! O hear my call,
And guard and save me from them all !

EVEN-SONG.

 COME to Thee to-night,
   In my lone closet where no eye can
      see,
And dare to crave communion high with Thee,
   Father of love and light!

   Softly the moonbeams shine
On the still branches of the shadowy trees,
While all sweet sounds of evening on the breeze
   Steal through the slumbering vine.

   Thou gavest the calm repose
That rests on all,—the air, the birds, the
      flowers,
The human spirit in its weary hours,
   Now at the bright day's close.

   'T is Nature's time for prayer;
The silent praises of the glorious sky,
And the earth's orisons, profound and high,
   To Heaven their breathings bear.

With them my soul would bend
In humble reverence at Thy holy throne,
Trusting the merits of Thy Son alone
        Thy sceptre to extend.

        If I this day have striven
With Thy blest Spirit, or have bowed the knee
To aught of earth in weak idolatry,
        I pray to be forgiven.

        If I have turned away
From grief or suffering which I might relieve,
Careless the cup of water e'en to give,
        Forgive me, Lord, I pray.

        And teach me how to feel
My sinful wanderings with a deeper smart;
And more of mercy and of grace impart,
        My sinfulness to heal.

        Not for myself alone
Would I these blessings of Thy love implore;
But for each penitent the wide world o'er,
        Whom Thou hast called Thine own.

        And for my heart's best friends,
Whose steadfast kindness o'er my painful years

Has watched to soothe affliction's grief and tears,
　My warmest prayer ascends.

　Should o'er their path decline
The light of gladness, or of hope, or health,
Be Thou their solace, and their joy, and wealth,
　As they have long been mine.

　And now, O Father, take
The heart I cast with humble faith on Thee,
And cleanse its depths from each impurity,
　For my Redeemer's sake!

19

LIGHTEN OUR DARKNESS.

GOD the Father, be Thou near,
  Save from every harm to-night;
Make us all Thy children dear,
In the darkness be our Light.

God the Saviour, be our Peace,
  Put away our sins to-night;
Speak the word of full release,
  Turn our darkness into light.

Holy Spirit, deign to come,
  Sanctify us all to-night;
In our hearts prepare Thy home,
  Then our darkness shall be light.

Holy Trinity, be nigh!
  Mystery of love adored,
Help to live and help to die,—
  Lighten all our darkness, Lord!

AN EVENING HYMN.

SWEET Saviour! bless us ere we go ;
   Thy word into our minds instil ;
   And make our lukewarm hearts to glow
With lowly love and fervent will.
Through life's long day and death's dark night,
O gentle Jesus! be our light !

The day is done, its hours have run ;
   And Thou hast taken count of all, —
The scanty triumphs grace hath won,
   The broken vow, the frequent fall.

Grant us, dear Lord! from evil ways
   True absolution and release ;
And bless us more than in past days
   With purity and inward peace.

Do more than pardon ; give us joy,
   Sweet fear, and sober liberty ;
And simple hearts without alloy
   That only long to be like Thee.

 Elim, or Hymns

Labor is sweet, for Thou hast toiled ;
  And care is light, for Thou hast cared :
Ah ! never let our works be soiled
  With strife, or by deceit ensnared.

For all we love, the poor, the sad,
  The sinful, —— unto Thee we call ;
O let Thy mercy make us glad :
  Thou art our Jesus and our All !
Through life's long day and death's dark night,
O gentle Jesus ! be our light !

MIDNIGHT.

MY God, now I from sleep awake,
The sole possession of me take ;
From midnight terrors me secure,
And guard my heart from thoughts impure !

Bless'd angels ! while we silent lie,
You hallelujahs sing on high ;
You joyful hymn the Ever-blest
Before the throne, and never rest.

I with your choir celestial join
In offering up a hymn divine ;
With you in heaven I hope to dwell,
And bid the night and world farewell.

Give me a place at Thy saints' feet,
Or some fall'n angel's vacant seat !
I 'll strive to sing as loud as they
Who sit above in brighter day.

O may I always ready stand
With my lamp burning in my hand :

May I in sight of Heaven rejoice,
Whene'er I hear the Bridegroom's voice!

The Sun in its meridian height
Is very darkness in Thy sight!
My soul O lighten and inflame,
With thought and love of Thy great Name!

Bless'd Jesu, Thou on heaven intent,
Whole nights hast in devotion spent;
But I, frail creature, soon am tired,
And all my zeal is soon expired.

Lord, lest the tempter me surprise,
Watch over Thine own sacrifice!
All loose, all idle thoughts cast out,
And make my very dreams devout!

Praise God, from whom all blessings flow;
Praise Him, all creatures here below!
Praise Him above, ye heavenly host;
Praise Father, Son, and Holy Ghost!

MORNING.

COME, my soul, thou must be waking :
Now is breaking
O'er the earth another day :
Come to Him who made this splendor,
See thou render
All thy feeble strength can pay.

Gladly hail the light returning :
Ready burning
Be the incense of thy powers :
For the night is safely ended ;
God hath tended
With His care thy helpless hours.

Pray that He may prosper ever
Each endeavor,
When thine aim is good and true ;
But that He may ever thwart thee
And convert thee,
When thou evil would'st pursue.

Think that He thy ways beholdeth,
He unfoldeth
 Every fault that lurks within,
Every stain of shame glossed over
Can discover,
 And discern each deed of sin.

Fettered to the fleeting hours,
All our powers,
 Vain and brief are borne away :
Time, my soul, thy ship is steering,
Onward veering,
 To the gulf of death a prey.

Only God's free gifts abuse not,
Light refuse not,
 But His Spirit's voice obey ;
Soon shall joy thy brow be wreathing,
Splendor breathing
 Fairer than the fairest day.

PRAYER FOR THE GIFT OF GRATITUDE.

OH, come to me, dear Lord, I pray,
And let Thy love my spirit stay :
Behold, it longeth sore for Thee,
I would it might more worthy be.
To forest streams the hart doth hie,
When he for thirst is fain to die ;
And so my soul doth pant for Thee,
O Jesu, Jesu, come to me.

I cannot love Thee as I would,
Yet pardon me, O Highest Good ;
My life, and all I call mine own,
I lay before Thine altar-throne :
And if a thousand lives were mine,
O sweetest Lord, they should be Thine ;
And scanty would the offering be,
So richly hast Thou loved me.

IN ALL TIME OF OUR PROSPERITY GOOD
LORD DELIVER US.

OH, not alone when blinding tears
    Fall over those we 've lately lost,
    And our weak hearts are wrecked and
       tossed
On the dark ocean of our fears ; —

But when dear friends around us prove
    How sweet the joys that Thou hast given,
    Then, lest we lose our hold on heaven,
Good Lord, deliver in Thy love !

Not only when the weary head
    Turns restlessly through all the night,
    And watches, longing, till the light
Comes, joyless, to the sufferer's bed ; —

But when, with even pulse, the blood
    Thrills through our veins unchecked and free,
    Then, lest we fail in love to Thee,
Dear Lord, deliver, — Thou art good !

Not only when in poverty
  We sink beneath our load of care,
  And drag the Cross we cannot bear,
As did our Lord on Calvary ; —

But when the stores of wealth are poured,
  Around us by Thy liberal grace,
  Lest what Thou givest hide Thy face,
Oh then deliver us, good Lord !

Not only when, with faltering tread,
  We totter down the slope of age,
  And, weary with our pilgrimage,
Envy the sweetly slumbering dead ; —

But when we raise the battle-song,
  In youth's glad hour of hope and pride,
  Then, lest we leave our Captain's side,
Kind Lord, deliver, — Thou art Strong.

Our sorrows guide us to Thy feet,
  We seek Thee through the gathering cloud,
  And when the tempest thunders loud,
We hide beneath the mercy-seat.

But joy oft leads us far astray,
    We value not Thy strong defence ;
    Oh seek us where we wander thence,
Good Lord, deliver then, we pray.

ASPIRATION.

OH Lord, my God, how long I for the day
  When this poor, doubting, sinful heart
  Shall ne'er be vexed by Satan's art,
But throughly cleansed from all impurity ;
    When shall it be ?

Joyful I tread Thy courts ; I love them well :
  Yet my heart pineth to behold
  The pearly gates and streets of gold,
And shall I *ever* that fair city see ?
    When shall it be ?

Ofttimes I feel a secret worm within
  Stealthily gnawing at life's inmost core,
  And a still voice asks daily, o'er and o'er :
" Is the dread Reaper sent to gather me ? "
    When shall it be ?

Now do I see how life goes out in pining,
  While death, impatient, waits his prey :

Quickly night shutteth out the day ;
Then work and prayer are over, soul, for thee :
Soon shall it be ?

O Lord, my God ! I ask not rest ; but only
That morn and eve to Thee I bring
A broken heart for offering ;
Waiting till Thou shalt please to set it free,
Then let it be !

DAY AND NIGHT.

" It is a good thing to give thanks unto the Lord, and to sing praises unto Thy Name, O most Highest; To tell of Thy loving-kindness early in the morning; and of Thy Truth in the night-season. — Psalm xcii. 1, 2.

THINK of Thee, my God, by night,
    And talk of Thee by day ;
Thy love my treasure and delight,
Thy truth my strength and stay.

The day is dark, the night is long,
    Unblest with thoughts of Thee ;
And dull to me the sweetest song
    Unless its theme Thou be.

Like pleasant thoughts of those we love,
    Which are of self a part,
Which neither day nor night remove
    Out of the loving heart, —

So all day long, and all the night,
  Lord, let Thy presence be
Mine air, my breath, my shade, my light,
  Myself absorbed in Thee.

DISCOURAGED BECAUSE OF THE WAY.

HE way seems dark about me ; overhead
The clouds have long since met in
gloomy spread,
And when I looked to see the day break through,
Cloud after cloud came up with volume new.

And in that shadow I have passed along,
Feeling myself grow weak as it grew strong,
Walking in doubt, and searching for the way,
And often at a stand, as now to-day.

And if before me on the path there lies
A spot of brightness from imagined skies,
Imagined shadows fall across it, too,
And the far future takes the present hue.

Perplexities'do throng upon my sight,
Like scudding fog-banks, to obscure the light ;

Some new dilemma rises every day,
And I can only shut my eyes and pray.

Lord, I am not sufficient for these things ;
Give me the light that Thy sweet presence
    brings ;
Give me Thy grace ; give me Thy constant
    strength ;
Lord, for my comfort, now appear at length.

It may be that my way doth seem confused,
Because my heart of Thy way is afraid, —
Because my eyes have constantly refused
To see the only opening Thou hast made.

Because my will would cross some flowery plain,
Where Thou hast thrown a hedge from every
    side,
And turneth from the stony walk of pain,
Its trouble or its care not even tried.

If thus I try to force my way along,
The smoothest road incumbered is for me ;
For were I as an angel swift and strong,
I could not go unless allowed by Thee.

And now I pray Thee, Lord, to lead Thy child,
Poor wretched wanderer from Thy grace and
    love, —
Whatever way Thou pleasest through the wild,
So it but take me to Thy home above.

Laboro.

THE MAID IN SYRIA.

"WHO for the like of me will care?"
　　So whispers many a mournful heart,
　　When in the weary languid air
For grief or scorn we pine apart.

So haply mus'd yon little maid,
　　From Israel's breezy mountains borne,
No more to rest in Sabbath shade,
　　Watching the free and wavy corn.

A captive now, and sold and bought,
　　In the proud Syrian's hall she waits,
Forgotten, — such her moody thought, —
　　Even as the worm beneath the gates.

But One who ne'er forgets is here:
　　He hath a word for thee to speak:
Oh, serve Him yet in duteous fear,
　　And to thy Gentile lord be meek.

So shall the healing Name be known
  By thee on many a heathen shore,
And Naaman on his chariot throne
  Wait humbly by Elisha's door.

By thee desponding lepers know
  The sacred water's sevenfold might,
Then wherefore sink in listless woe?
  Christ's poor and needy claim your right.

Your heavenly right, to do and bear
  All for His sake; nor yield one sigh
To pining doubt; nor ask "What care
  In the wide world for such as I?"

ONE BY ONE.

ONE by one the sands are flowing,
   One by one the moments fall;
   Some are coming, some are going,
Do not strive to grasp them all.

One by one thy duties wait thee,
   Let thy whole strength go to each;
Let no future dreams elate thee,
   Learn thou first what these can teach.

One by one, bright gifts from Heaven,
   Joys are sent thee here below;
Take them readily when given,
   Ready, too, to let them go.

One by one thy griefs shall meet thee:
   Do not fear an armèd band;
One will fade as others reach thee,
   Shadows passing through the land.

Do not look at life's long sorrow,
   See how small each moment's pain;

God will help thee for to-morrow,
   Every day begin again.

Every hour that fleets so slowly
   Has its task to do, or bear;
Luminous the crown, and holy,
   If thou set each gem with care.

Do not linger with regretting,
   Or for passing hours despond;
Nor, the daily toil forgetting,
   Look too eagerly beyond.

Hours are golden links, God's token
   Reaching Heaven; but one by one
Take them, lest the chain be broken
   Ere the pilgrimage be done.

THEY THAT SOW IN TEARS SHALL REAP IN JOY.

YE have not sowed in vain!
 Though the heavens seem as brass,
 And piercing the crust of the burning
  plain
Ye scan not a blade of grass.

Yet there is life within,
 And waters of life on high;
One morn ye shall wake, and the Spring's soft
  green
 O'er the moistened fields shall lie.

Tears in the dull, cold eye,
 Light on the darkened brow,
The smile of peace, or the prayerful sigh,
 Where the mocking smile sits now.

Went ye not forth with prayer?
 Then ye went not forth in vain;
" The Sower, the Son of man," was there,
 And His was that precious grain.

Ye may not see the bud,
  The first sweet sign of Spring,
The first slow drops of the quickening showe.
  On the dry, hard ground that ring.

But the harvest-home ye 'll keep,
  The Summer of life ye 'll share,
When they that sow and they that reap
  Rejoice together *there*.

CHRIST AT SYCHAR.

" Jesus saith unto her, Give Me to drink." — St. John iv. 7.

GIVE Me to drink! And who and what art Thou
    That askest drink of me, a child of earth ?
O wondrous suppliant! Yes, I know Thee now,
  Though once a stranger to Thy matchless worth.

Give Thee to drink! Yes, had I seen Thee here
    Athirst and weary, seated on the well,
O how mine heart had throbbed Thine heart to cheer,
  This feeble tongue it hath no words to tell.

But Jesus say — what wouldst Thou have me do
    To prove the love I *then* would fain have showed ?

"I have a little band, a faithful few,
   Pilgrims and strangers on their homeward
      road.

" Whene'er you see *them* weary on the way,
   Athirst or fainting, *then* remember Me;
Think then thou hearest Me, the Master, say,
   'Give Me to drink.'   This boon I crave of
      thee.

" And, oh! when thou shalt sit with Me beside
   The river of life's water, cool and clear,
The same which issued from My wounded side,
   When in death's agony I thirsted here,

"I will give thee to drink — oh! such a draught
   Of life and love from My unbounded store,
As no poor thirsting spirit ever quaffed,
   When thou shalt drink with Me and thirst
      no more."

THE SAGES AND THE SHEPHERDS.

CAME North and South and East and
   West,
   Four sages, to a mountain crest,
Each pledged to search the wide world round
Until the wondrous well he found.

Before a crag they made their seat,
Pure bubbling waters at their feet.
Said one, This well is small and mean,
Too petty for a village green !
Another said, So small and dumb,
From earth's deep centre can it come ?
The third, This water seems not rare,
Not even bright, but pale as air !
The fourth, Thick crowds I looked to see ;
Where the true well is these must be.

They rose and left the mountain crest, —
One North, one South, one East, one West.
O'er many seas and deserts wide
They wandered, thirsting, till they died.

The simple shepherds by the mountain dwell,
And dip their pitchers in the wondrous well.

"AS ONE WHOM HIS MOTHER COM-
FORTETH."

I COME, dear Lord, like a tired child, to creep
Unto Thy feet, and there awhile to sleep.
Weary, though not with a long busy day,
But with the morning's sunshine and with play,
And with some tears that fell, although, the while,
They scarce were deep enough to drown a smile.

There is no need of words of mine to tell
My heart to Thee; Thou needest not to spell,
As others must, my hidden thoughts and fears,
From out my broken words, my sobs, or tears;
Thou knowest all, knowest far more than I,
The inner meaning of each tear or sigh.

Thou mayest smile, perchance, as mothers smile
On sobbing children, seeing, all the while,

How soon will pass away the endless grief,
How soon will come the gladness and relief;
But if Thou smilest, yet Thy sympathy
Measures my grief by what it is to me.

And not the less Thy love doth understand,
And not the less, with tender, pitying hand,
Thou wipest all my tears, and the sad face
Doth cherish to a smile in Thy embrace,
Until the pain is gone, and Thou dost say,
" Go now, my child, and work for Me to-day."

21

SOMETHING FOR THEE.

SOMETHING, my God, for Thee,
    Something for Thee ;
  That each day's setting sun may bring
Some penitential offering ;
In Thy dear name some kindness done ;
To Thy dear love some wanderer won ;
Some trial meekly borne for Thee,
    Dear Lord, for Thee.

Something, my God, for Thee,
    Something for Thee ;
That to Thy gracious throne may rise
Sweet incense from some sacrifice, —
Uplifted eyes undimmed by tears,
Uplifted faith unstained by fears,
Hailing each joy as light from Thee,
    Dear Lord, from Thee.

Something, my God, for Thee,
    Something for Thee ;
For the great love that Thou hast given,
For the great hope of Thee and heaven,
My soul her first allegiance brings,
And upward plumes her heavenward wings,
" Nearer, my God, to Thee,
    Nearer to Thee ! "

THE CARVER'S LESSON.

RUST me, no mere skill of subtle
   tracery,
   No mere practice of a dextrous hand,
Will suffice without a hidden spirit,
   That we may or may not understand.

And those quaint old fragments that are left us
   Have their power in this, — the artist brought
Earnest faith and reverent patience only
   Worthily to clothe some noble thought.

Shut there in the petals of the flowers,
   Round the stems of all the lilies twine,
Hide beneath the bird's or angel's pinions,
   Some wise meaning or some thought divine.

Place in stony hands, that pray forever,
   Tender words of peace ; and strive to bind
Round the leafy scrolls and fretted niches
   Some true loving message to your kind.

Some will praise, some blame, and some for-
     getting,
  Come and go, nor even pause to gaze ;
Only now and then a passing stranger
  Just may linger, with a word of praise.

But I think, when years have floated onward,
  And the stone is gray and dim and old,
And the hand forgotten that had carved it,
  And the heart that dreamt it still and cold, —

There may come some weary soul, o'erladen
  With perplexing trouble of the brain,
Or, it may be, fretted with life's turmoil,
  Or made sore by some perpetual pain ; —

Then I think those stony hands will open,
  And the gentle lilies overflow
With the blessing and the loving token
  That you hid there many years ago.

And those tendrils will unfold, and teach him
  How to solve the problem of his pain,
And those birds' and angels' wings shake down-
     ward
  On his head a meek and quiet rain.

While he marvels at his fancy finding
  Meaning in that quaint and ancient scroll,
Little guessing that the loving carver
  Left the lesson for his weary soul.

MARAH AND ELIM.

Exodus xv. 23–27.

TO-DAY 't is Elim, with its palms and
     wells,
    And happy shade for desert-weariness;
'T was Marah yesterday, all rock and sand,
    Unshaded solitude and bitterness.

Yet the same desert holds them both ; the same
    Soft breezes wander o'er the lonely ground ;
The same low stretch of valley shelters both,
    And the same mountains. compass them
     around.

So is it here with us on earth ; and so
    I do remember it has ever been ;
The bitter and the sweet, the grief and joy,
    Lie near together, but a day between.

Sometimes God turns our bitter into sweet ;
    Sometimes He gives us pleasant water-
     springs ;

Sometimes He shades us with His pillar-cloud,
　And sometimes to a blessed palm-shade brings.

What matters it ? The time will not be long ; —
　Marah and Elim will alike be past ;
Our desert-wells and palms will soon be done ;
　We reach the city of our God at last.

O happy land ! beyond these lonely hills,
　Where gush in joy the everlasting springs ;
O holy Paradise ! above these heavens,
　Where we shall end our desert-wanderings.

INDEX OF FIRST LINES.

	Page
Ah many a time we look on starlit nights	197
Alleluia! Alleluia!	158
A pathway opens from the tomb	160
Art thou weary? art thou languid?	71
Behind them lies the desert waste	38
Behold! a Stranger's at the door!	46
Brief life is here our portion	263
By Christ redeemed, in Christ restored	186
By Nebo's lonely mountain	203
Calm lay the city in its double sleep	141
Came North and South and East and West	319
Come, Lord, and tarry not	181
Come, Lord Jesus, quickly come!	180
Come, my soul, thou must be waking	295
Come, O Thou Traveller unknown	57
Come! ye lofty, come! ye lowly	87
Cross, most adored! to thee I give my heart	123
Darker than night, life's shadows fall around us	18
Darkly rose the guilty morning	98
Dear little One! how sweet Thou art	89
Dear Saviour of a dying world	235
Down below the wild November whistling	248
Faith is a very slender thing	219
Far from the Shepherd's one true Fold I stray	229

	Page
Father ! for Thy kindest word	11
Father, my cup is full !	102
Father of Love, who didst not spare	169
For all who in Thy steadfast faith	201
Forth from the city gate	238
Fresh glides the brook and blows the gale	199
From England's gilded halls of state	194
From tangled ways by which I wandered far	7
Give Me to drink ! And who and what art Thou	317
God the Father, be Thou near	290
Hark the sound of holy voices	212
He cometh, on yon hallowed Board	145
Here is my heart !— my God, I give it Thee	281
Here, O my Lord, I see Thee face to face	136
Here on earth, where foes surround us	55
How long, O Lord, in weariness and sorrow	174
I ask not wealth, but power to take	278
I bore with thee long weary days and nights	34
I come, dear Lord, like a tired child, to creep	320
I come, O Lord, to Thy dear face	109
I come to Thee to-night	287
I do not ask, O Lord, that Thou shouldst shed	280
I have a heritage of joy	270
In the silent midnight watches	224
In those dark hours of bitter woe	107
I saw again. Behold ! Heaven's open door	207
I think of Thee, my God, by night	303
I thirst, Thou wounded Lamb of God	119
It is a day of fear	134
I would that I were fairer, Lord !	82
Jesu ! behold, the Wise from far	36

PAGE

Jesu! guide our way 171
Jesu, mighty Sufferer! say . . . 96
Jesus is God! the glorious bands . . . 53
Jesus, pro me perforatus . . . 152
Jesus, Thou Joy of loving hearts!. . . 23
Jesus, while He dwelt below . . . 104

Lead, kindly Light, amid the encircling gloom . 190
Left in her little room alone . . . 244
Lift up your heads, ye mighty gates . . 167
Lord Jesus Christ, my faithful Shepherd, hear . 233
Lord, to Thine altar let me go . . . 133
Lord, what unvalued pleasures crowned . 284
Lo! the feast is spread to-day . . . 132
Love craves the presence and the sight . . 215
Love, in all its depth and height . . . 69
Love's tears fell fast, like the thick rain that weepeth 241

Master, where abidest Thou? . . . 28
My God, now I from sleep awake . . 293
Mysterious is Thy presence, Lord . . . 127

No Gospel like this Feast . . . 148
Not from Jerusalem alone . · . . 256
Now lift the carol, men and maids . . 94

O'er the distant mountains breaking . . 183
Oh, come to me, dear Lord, I pray . . 297
Oh Lord, my God, how long I for the day . . 301
Oh, not alone when blinding tears . . 298
O Lord, the wilderness to me . . . 40
O Love, who formedst me to wear . . 73
O Mount beloved! mine eyes again . . 16
Once I thought to sit so high . . . 130
One by one the sands are flowing . . . 313

              PAGE

One Priest alone can pardon me . . . 231
One sweetly solemn thought . . . 252
Only waiting till the shadows . . . 259
On red Rephidim's battle-plain . . 191
O time of tranquil joy and holy feeling! . 44
Out on the world, unheeded, came there One at
  midnight hour 91

Perpetual peace flows from that word . . 80

Rejoice, rejoice, believers! . . . 176
Resting from His work to-day . . 156
Rest, weary heart 49

Say, art thou wounded, feeble, weak? . . 75
She brought her box of alabaster . . . 222
Silence in the house of prayer . . . 154
Something, my God, for Thee . . 322
Soon will the heavenly Bridegroom come . 184
Supreme High-Priest, the pilgrim's light . . 68
Sweet Saviour! bless us ere we go . . 291

That I am Thine, my Lord and God! . . 51
The Apostle slept, — a light shone in the prison 254
The day is past and over 286
The Galilean fishers toil . . . 32
" The Master has come over Jordan " . . 62
The merry world did, on a day . . . 78
The night is far spent, and the day is at hand . 172
There is an everlasting home . . . 121
There is a rapturous movement, a green growing . 100
There is no night in heaven . . . 268
There was a ship, one eve autumnal, onward . 3
The rocky path still climbs the glowing steep . 20
The sick man in his chamber . . . 226

PAGE

The sun is sinking in the west . . . 125
The tomb is empty; wouldst thou have it full ? . 162
The way seems dark about me; overhead . 305
The wise men to Thy cradle throne . . 48
The wonder-working Master . . . 85
The world against me, I against the world . 217
They are going — only going . . . 261
They have stopped the sacred well which the Patri-
    archs dug of old , . . 30
They talked of Jesus, as they went . . 42
This earth is the court of a palace . . 271
Thou art, O God, my East! In Thee I dawned . 15
Thou Bread of Life, upon Thy tongue . 129
Thou didst love the evening hours . . . 275
Thou knowest, Lord, the weariness and sorrow 25
Thou passest by — Thy awful step I hear . 76
Thou, that on the first of Easters . . . 165
Through miry paths I labored on . . 115
Through my life, Thy spirit striving . . 9
Through paths of pleasant thought I ran . 1
To-day 't is Elim, with its palms and wells . 327
True Bread of life, in pitying mercy given . 139
Trust me, no mere skill of subtle tracery . . 324

Weary, working, plodding one . . . 114
We have no home on earth below . . . 247
Were it from my heart alone . . . 150
We were not with the faithful few . . . 6
"We would see Jesus;" for the shadows lengthen 83
What countless crowd on Sion stands ? . 210
What time the Saviour spread His feast . 59
When across the inward thought . . 188
When across the heart deep waves of sorrow . 117
When apple-blossoms in the spring . . 13
When Jesus came to earth of old . . . 178

	PAGE
When languor and disease invade	65
When the house doth sigh and weep	187
When, wounded sore, the stricken soul	112
"Who for the like of me will care?"	311
With all the powers my poor soul hath	143
Ye have not sowed in vain.	315